Comanche Dawn

Out chasing outlaws Texas Ranger Cal Avery comes across a wrecked stagecoach, and a dead man and woman nearby. In a gully, under a juniper bush, lies another young woman, thrown clear when the coach went over and who cannot remember anything.

When a cavalry supply train comes along with Avery's old friend, Jumbo Jepson, as the lead teamster, he decides that travelling with them is the best course of action. But in Cal's absence, unscrupulous Indian Agent, Jake Elkins, has bribed men to swear that Cal has gunned down two innocent men in cold blood, and now there is a warrant out for his arrest.

The travellers must head for the safety of Fort Griffin, avoiding the pursuing Indians, and the corrupt law, who are trying to halt their progress. . . .

Comanche Dawn

Jake Shipley

A Black Horse Western

ROBERT HALE · LONDON

ISBN 978-0-7198-1232-3

Robert Hale Limited
Clerkenwell House
Clerkenwell Green
London EC1R 0HT

www.halebooks.com

Typeset by
Derek Doyle & Associates, Shaw Heath
Printed and bound in Great Britain by
CPI Antony Rowe, Chippenham and Eastbourne

1

Her dust-caked eyes blinked involuntarily as a fierce Texas wind whipped across the open range, bending all but the most solidly founded objects to its unrelenting will. Sagebrush, small branches and leaves flew unfettered in the sandy dust to crash against the scattering of rocky outcrops.

Near a group of craggy boulders, in a shallow gully barely eighteen inches deep, under a dense juniper bush, a young woman stirred as though waking from a dream. She tried to lift a weak hand to rub some feeling into her eyes, pain shot up her leaden arm when she tried to raise it. The inside of her head was as muzzy as a marshmallow. Even in the semi-shade of the juniper bush the harsh glare of the sun hurt. Flies, buzzing annoyingly, seemed to be everywhere.

Each time she tried to open her eyes the intensity of the daylight forced them shut, tighter each time. Her body was regaining consciousness much faster than her confused brain. Where she was, who she was, what she was, she had no idea, only that she was alive, as testified by the pain that engulfed her entire body. A numbness hampered every muscle; every sinew; all but the slightest movement was out of the question. She knew she was powerless to change that. Exhaustion closed her eyes again, and she slept.

How long she slept she had no way of knowing, but when she opened her eyes even a fraction the blistering sun almost fried her eyeballs. It was like before, but this time somehow not as painful. She squinted, trying to look around, but all she could see was stony red earth. Bit by bit her senses slowly began to return. The pain was still there. Where was she hurt? Where *wasn't* she? her brain answered.

She sucked her bottom lip, her dry tongue dragging across the parched skin. A drink. She was desperate for a drink. That one thought consumed her: she had to move, find water, try to ignore the pain. She flexed her fingers; the back of her hand touched something sharp. She flinched, blinked once, twice, three times, her eyes were still not accustomed to the intense sunlight. *Where am I?* The question pounded repeatedly inside her head, but still she had no answer. Scrunching up her eyes, she tried to remember something, anything, but nothing came by way of an answer; she had no idea what had happened or how she came to be there. Her brain told her she was thirsty, to concentrate on finding a drink. Ignoring the pain she raised an aching hand to shield her eyes and tried to push herself more upright with her other elbow, instinctively stifling the scream of pain that fought to escape her lips. Somehow she knew she must stay quiet until she knew what dangers lurked near by.

As though by auto-suggestion she sensed that something living was close by. It was somewhere to her left, sniffing, breathing, panting. The frightening sounds came loud to her ears, amplified in the otherwise relative silence. At first her brain could not unravel the information being fed to it.

Through squinting eyes she saw lank fur. She flinched painfully, once again fighting back the scream that dried in her throat, wanting above all to cry out for help, but knowing it best to stay silent. More panting sounds came from behind her. Whatever they were, there must be at least two of them. Neither creature came into view; the panting grew louder now. She knew she had to move, and managed to turn her head slightly. She caught a glimpse of a furry tail. She had no notion of what this might signify, but recognized the danger signals flashing through her head. Another sound drifted to her ears – hoofbeats? A surge of hope filled her breast. Was it a horse? She prayed to God it was. Suddenly she realized that some memories had become clearer.

The hoofbeats came nearer. A fuzzy distant memory invaded her brain – one that signified danger. She clamped her eyes tighter, instinctively mouthing a silent prayer: *The Lord is my shepherd* – the words shuffled into her head. The hoofbeats had stopped, but not the sniffing and panting. Footfalls crunched on the parched earth, accompanied by a metallic jingling. She fought back her fear, almost swooning as the silent scream gagged once more in her throat.

Something cold and wet pressed against the skin on her bare shoulder, making her jump. She hadn't realized that the top of her dress had been torn away. She felt a wet tongue licking her tender skin. She held her breath, not daring to breathe.

Moments earlier, Cal Avery had reined in his horse on a small rise. There was smoke in the air; he had sniffed the acrid smell for a mile or so, his nostrils twitching. The ears of both his horses laid back, sensing something. Now he saw the reason. He checked his natural instinct to gallop down to take a closer look. In the near distance wisps of smoke drifted skyward on the light breeze. He raised his army telescope to his eye and scanned the flatlands before him for a movement or something out of place. He slipped the brass telescope back into his saddle-bag and flipped the rawhide thong off the hammer of his big Navy Colt. He drew the weapon, feeling the gun's perfect balance, he cocked and uncocked the piece, spun the chamber twice, then holstered the gun. Next he tugged the Winchester from its saddle holster, and levered a cartridge into the breech. Satisfied that his arsenal was fully loaded and in good working order he jogged the buckskin down the shallow incline on to even ground. A wave of his hand was the signal for the dogs to race ahead – they were the best forward scouts he'd ever had.

The Fort Worth to San Angelo stagecoach road ran along the valley floor, cutting across his intended path; Cal turned his horse towards the place where he had seen the smoke. His two dogs had already run on ahead.

Once around a rocky outcrop the sight that greeted him was no surprise – he had already guessed the origin of the smoke. Cal reined in the buckskin and stepped down.

The stagecoach was lying on its right side, its front axle shattered; probably it had hit a rock as the driver tried to veer from the rough track they called a road in these parts. He had probably been trying to make it to the clump of rocks away to the left. The team of horses were gone; the traces had been cleanly cut. He could see two bodies: one man, one woman. Debris lay scattered all around. A large brown valise lay open, clothes spilling over its sides. One or two garments lay near by, sad and discarded. Other trunks and boxes lay strewn across a wide area: all were open.

Cal's two dogs were sniffing around near the bodies. He pinged a stone across the shaly ground.

9

'Get away from there!' His shout echoed across the range. The second stone he threw ricocheted off a rock. 'Get away, I said!' Another stone kicked up a small cloud of dust near the dog's head. The big hound yelped and drew back. 'Get away, I told you.'

Cal ground-hitched his two horses and ambled over to the coach. He squatted down on his haunches to take a closer look at the unmoving body of a man. He pushed his hat further to the back of his head, hoping the man had died quick.

The man was still wearing one boot, the sole of which was well worn and torn away. Cal reflected: Indians had no use for a sole-less boot. The other boot was nowhere to be seen. On the bootless foot was a holey sock: two toes and the heel poked out. The man's gloveless hands were rough and heavily calloused in places where a man would have held the reins of a team of horses. Cal figured the man to have been the stagecoach driver. The man's wrists were burned black by the sun, in contrast to the skin on the back of his white hands, indicating that the man usually wore gloves. Cal ruminated on the conundrum: a driver and one woman? It was unusual for a stagecoach to be carrying only one passenger.

He sauntered over to where a broken rear coach wheel lay half-propped-up against the roof of the coach. The dead woman was leaning against it; Cal estimated she was in her mid-forties. An empty purse was tied to the woman's wrist with a thin crimson ribbon; her blistered lips testified to the searing heat of the day. Streaks of tears, now dried to a crust by the sun, had run down her once pleasant face.

A lump of feeling he hadn't thought himself still capable of rose from deep within to catch in his throat. Somebody's wife, or mother, or sweetheart. He shook away the vivid mental images from his mind's eye.

Cal eased her body to the ground, fetched a blanket from his bedroll and covered her.

Behind him the buckskin pawed the ground and snorted.

'Easy, boy. Easy.'

The voice was baritone-deep; the drawl Western.

The inside of the girl's head buzzed with another set of memories – English! And another – a white man's voice! Hope filled her heart. Painfully she raised herself a little higher, wishing she hadn't tried when the pain returned. The spur-jingling footsteps moved past where she lay. The dog! For a moment she had forgotten about the dog. More memories. A dog? At least it wasn't a wolf or coyote. More memories were returning.

Her hope-filled thoughts turned suddenly to fear: what if the man was a thief, a robber? A murderer or a Comanchero? She remembered the stories she had heard of men who were the worst kind of desperado.

Finding the strength to ignore the pain she pushed down hard with her elbows, edging further under the bush.

The outline of the man was now some distance away; her eyes were still not focusing clearly. Maybe he had seen her and thought she was dead. Then came sounds of wood scraping across wood, the occasional thud of something heavy hitting the hard earth. Things were being examined. But what? What was the man doing?

She needed to remember: try again to recall some memory of what had happened. The result was an even more painful headache. The hopelessness of her predicament ate away at her insides. It was no use. She had no choice but to show herself. To trust in the Good Lord to protect her; her faith would have to carry her through.

Moving even slightly brought a return of the excruciating pain. Should she cry out? Lord knows, she wanted to. Could she? She tried to call out but no sound came from her parched lips; her mouth was too dry.

Gritting her teeth she edged slowly forwards, pain shooting up her right arm, her elbow burning like fire when she touched it to the hard earth. Ignoring the painful thorns, she grasped hold of the sturdiest branch her fingers could find and tugged with all her might, simultaneously pushing her backside against the side of the depression. Slowly, inch by inch she moved her body out of her shelter towards the direct sunlight until her eyes peered above the rim of the shallow depression. The sun burned the skin on her face and shoulder. One or two blinks helped adjust her eyesight.

Long distances were still shrouded in a milky-grey cloud. Nearer objects were obscured by a shimmering heat haze. She peered around for some moments before her sight became clearer. Away to her left stood a horse: a big handsome buckskin, passive, patient. Behind the buckskin she saw a second horse: a big dun, packs on its back – a packhorse. To the right of the horses was what looked to be a stagecoach lying on its side. Had she been a passenger, she wondered? A jingling sound drew her eyes away from the clothing. The outline of a man hove into view.

She felt the bile rising painfully inside her. The acrid taste filled her mouth. She gagged, vomit springing uncontrolled from her mouth. She almost choked as she coughed and spluttered.

The man came alert in an instant, spinning round; a six-gun suddenly appeared in his right hand; she heard the hammer clicking back. Her view was obscure; the sun was right behind him, silhouetting his large frame against the crystal-clear blue sky.

She closed her eyes and allowed gravity to return her body to the bottom of the depression; she prayed again.

The sounds of the man's boots and spurs

thumped and jingled, and worst of all, grew louder. She bit her lip and held her breath; she knew he must have seen her: knew he would soon find her. There was no escape; she had seen his gun, his fast draw; he must be an outlaw. A more intense panic set in. She retched again, but nothing came up, only a griping pain that clawed at her insides. She risked a fear-laden squint. The sun had disappeared, darkness had replaced it. The man's long shadow covered her completely. One trembling hand flew painfully to her mouth, she held her breath, not daring to move a fraction more.

The sound of a six-gun hammer being released preceded his voice.

'Found a live one.'

It wasn't what she had expected to hear, but it was the last thing she heard as she passed out, spiralling down and down into the depths of a black bottomless pit.

2

Cal cradled the girl's head in one hand; she was petite, her hair glowed as though burnished in the sunshine, she was just about breathing.

'Miss. Miss,' he whispered as softly as he could.

The sound of a man's deep voice swam through her marshmallow brain; the voice had a soothing quality. She screwed up her eyes against the fierce light, wondering who was speaking to her.

'Miss.'

Her eyes blinked open, then closed. She flinched.

Cal looked at her. She was a pretty young thing despite the dust and grime covering her face. Small too, probably no more than five-foot-three or four, small boned, but shapely, like a small bird in his huge hands.

'It's OK. You're safe now,' Cal told her. 'Let's get you out of there.'

She felt strong hands lift her from her hiding-place; powerful arms held her. Suddenly she felt safe: safe in his strong arms for the first time since she had regained consciousness. Forgetting the pain she threw an arm around his neck; her other arm she could move hardly at all.

Cal looked around for a cool spot and decided upon the overturned stagecoach He carried her over to the shade of the coach and gently set her down, her back against the roof for some support.

She felt him drape something warm across her legs.

He fetched a cloth and his canteen, then dabbed at her scorched face.

Her hooded eyes half-opened, seeing her rescuer clearly for the first time. Cool water ran down her cheek: he was wiping her face with something damp.

'Water,' he said, lifting the canteen to her lips. 'Take a sip, rinse it around your mouth, then spit it out.' She did as he said. 'Not too much just yet.'

She looked into his strong features. He seemed to be smiling at her. It was a warm smile – a nice smile – a smile of reassurance. His stained, once dove-coloured Stetson was pushed back on his head revealing a shock of black hair, glistening with sweat. One thick lock of hair hung across his fore-head. The corners of his steely-grey eyes crinkled into lines – eyes that had seen long service beneath the glaring Texas sun. His rugged complexion was swarthy from years of hard riding against the scorching winds of the summer and the icy blizzards of winter – he was not young, she thought, but then again, neither was he old.

Under a khaki coat he wore a black leather waistcoat over a heavy brown flannel shirt, and well-worn stained buckskin leggings; his high boots dusty and scuffed. He moved his arm, exposing a silver badge pinned to his chest over his heart; the badge glinted in the sunshine.

'How do you feel?' Cal asked, trying to keep his voice almost a whisper.

It was a nice voice, educated, dignified. She relaxed, allowing the tension in her muscles to slip away.

'Better,' she croaked.

Cal dabbed more water on her lips, gently wiping away the sweaty dust that had gathered at the corners of her mouth. He raised the canteen to her lips.

'Take another sip,' he told her. 'Rinse it around your mouth like before.' Again, she obeyed his suggestion. 'Now spit it out.'

She pushed away all thoughts of ladylike convention and spat out the crud-filled water.

'Good,' he said, 'now you can take a longer pull.'

She swallowed the tepid liquid with some difficulty, coughing. The water tasted slightly metallic, but she was grateful for its thirst-quenching qualities. She gulped down another mouthful, then coughed most of it up, spitting some over the man.

'Best to sip it.' He frowned, brushing droplets of water from his face and neck.

'Sorry,' she spluttered out, feeling embarrassed.

'Tell me what happened.'

The muscles in her face tightened as she tried to get her brain working. 'I . . . I can't remember,' she stammered.

Cal shrugged the tiniest of shrugs. 'What's your name?'

She took another sip from the canteen, thinking long and hard.

'I don't know.' The significance of her words suddenly hit her. 'I can't remember!' she said loudly. 'I can't remember!' She dropped the canteen and gripped his arm. Tears flooded her eyes.

Cal scooped up the canteen before too much water had spilled out. 'It'll come back to you. I've seen it before. Many times. Shock, the doctors call it.' His words and tone were reassuring, but held no emotion. Her eyes filled with fear, so he placed a hand on hers.

'You were lucky,' he told her. 'Must have been thrown clear when the coach flipped.' Cal made a flipping motion with his hand to emphasize his words. 'Yes, sir, you were mighty lucky to have ended up under that juniper where I found you. *Mighty* lucky,' he repeated fervently. He took off his coat and draped it round her shoulders. 'Be back in a minute,' he promised.

The dogs reacted first: both lay down, ears back, noses pointed in the direction of the movement. His horses sensed it too: they snorted, ears laid back like those of the dogs. Cal Avery had learned long ago to respect the instincts of his animals. He stood, one hand shielding his eyes, and scanned the ridge to the west, his gaze searching for any sign of danger. He paused once or twice when some tiny movement caught his attention.

The girl looked at him, suddenly realizing how tall he was: he must be well over six feet, broad at the chest and shoulder, narrow at the hip. She watched him walk away towards his horses, sure-footed, long-striding, deliberate in his every movement. He returned with a pair of leather saddle-bags.

'Hungry?' he asked her. She shook her head. 'You should try to eat something,' Cal told her.

She watched him take a bite out of something dark brown; it looked disgusting.

'Try some?' he offered.

'What is it?' She asked.

'Jerky. Dried beef,' he added, suddenly feeling the need to expand his reply. He held a piece out to her.

She smelled the jerky, and turned up her nose. 'I would rather not,' she said.

'Suit yourself.' He shrugged.

She knew from his reaction that her refusal had not pleased him. 'Sorry,' she said, 'I really am

19

grateful to you.'

Cal shrugged again, but didn't respond. He couldn't think of anything good to say, if truth be told.

She gestured towards the bodies. 'Are they dead?'

Cal nodded sombrely.

'We need to bury them,' she said.

He nodded his agreement. 'I'll take you as far as Camp Sheldon.'

'That would be kind of you,' she answered politely. She had no idea where Camp Sheldon was.

'No trouble. I'm heading that way anyhow. Any of this other luggage yours?'

'I . . . I'm not sure.'

'Let's take a look. See if you recognize anything.' Cal dragged a piece of the scattered luggage to a spot near the girl. Her eyes showed no recognition. 'Any memories come back?' Cal asked encouragingly.

She shook her head. 'Nothing. Sorry,' she added.

He carried over a large brown trunk; the lid swung limply from side to side, hanging from one damaged hinge.

'Here,' he said, setting the trunk on the ground in front of her. 'Take a look through these things. See if there's anything that looks familiar.' He turned the trunk on to its side to make it easier for her.

Cal left her sifting through the contents of the trunk, and went to bury the bodies. He had already decided to make use of the shallow ditch where he had found the girl.

It was a laborious, sweaty task, the sandy earth was hard and dusty. Satisfied with the depth of the makeshift graves, Cal fetched the woman's body which he had wrapped in a cloak, and set it down gently in the ditch that he had deepened.

He went back to get the second body, lifting the driver's lifeless corpse and carrying it to the makeshift grave. He laid the limp figure down alongside the dead woman, removing the dead man's single boot – a man shouldn't be buried wearing one boot, he decided. It was then that he noticed something he hadn't seen earlier. The driver's sock had worked its way down the ankle exposing the top of a grubby piece of folded paper. Cal fished it out. It was the stage-line manifest.

At the top were listed the names of the driver: Zebulon Fish and the shotgun guard, Buck Kilgallon. The manifest confirmed Cal's belief that there would most likely have been more passengers. There had been six in all; five females and one male.

He read the names of the women: Mrs Audrey Worsfold; Mrs Frieda Schwartz; Mrs Helen Baker; Mrs Dora Key, and Miss Amy Jordan. The man was listed as Sergeant Groves. Only the bodies of the driver and one woman were still at the scene; the others had most likely been taken captive.

One part of the mystery being resolved, Cal

tucked the manifest into his trouser pocket, and shovelled earth over the bodies; then he fetched two good-sized stones to place on the disturbed soil. At the head of the grave he constructed a small cairn. Not large enough to draw attention but recognizable to anyone searching for the location of the grave. Mopping the sweat from his brow, he stepped back a pace, satisfied with his work. The grave was partially hidden from casual view by the overhanging branches of the juniper bush.

He returned to the girl. 'I may have solved the mystery of your name.'

She looked up, puzzled at his words. 'What?' she asked.

He held out the manifest; she took it from him.

'Your name's most likely Miss Amy Jordan,' he told her.

She regarded the list of names, her eyes betraying no tinge of recognition. 'There are five female names on this list. How can you be sure which is mine?'

Cal squatted down on his haunches. 'Miss, I'm no detective, but the other names are of married women. You are not wearing a wedding ring.'

She lifted her left hand wearily, examining each finger: no rings, no sign of there ever having been one. She smiled thinly.

'So, I am Amy Jordan,' she said, raising her eyes to regard her rescuer. She was happy to have discovered her identity, and that she could read.

'Seems likely.' Cal smiled. 'Can you ride?' he asked her.

She hesitated, there was more than a hint of impatience in his deep voice. 'I . . . I think so,' she replied hesitantly.

'Good,' Cal said. 'We need to get away from here,' he told her. 'You take my horse. I'll ride the packhorse.'

She felt his powerful hands under her armpits. He lifted her as if she was a feather. As he released his grip she tottered for a second, then her leg gave way. She screamed.

'My ankle,' she called out.

He caught her before she could fall. Tears of pain showed clear in her eyes. He sat her down on a wooden packing case.

'Let's take a look.' He raised her face, seeking her approval to raise the hem of her skirt. This was no time for false modesty. She gritted her teeth and tugged up the skirt, exposing her stockinged leg up to the knee.

It was a shapely leg – not lost on Cal.

She gasped when she saw how her ankle had ballooned.

'Shoe needs to come off,' he said bluntly, his tone matter-of-fact.

She nodded, resting her hands on his broad shoulders to brace herself for what was to follow.

His touch was surprisingly gentle and confident. She bit her lip to fight the pain that shot up her leg as he whipped off the shoe in one sudden movement. Her fingernails dug deep into his shoulder to suppress the scream that fought to escape from her lips.

'I'll need to cut off your stocking.' He reached behind him and withdrew a long Bowie knife; the blade glinted in the harsh sunlight. He lifted her already discoloured foot and rested it on his knee. The razor-sharp blade sliced easily through the thin material of the stocking. His big strong hands, though rough, wrapped a strip of cloth he'd dampened with water from his canteen around her wound.

'Thank you,' she said warmly. She looking deep into his eyes, trying to discover more about the man who had proved to be her saviour.

Cal Avery was a modest, uncomplicated, unassuming man of dignified demeanour; tough, hardy, he was well qualified for his chosen branch of law enforcement. He was daring, quick to act, and cool under pressure. All prized attributes in his job as a Texas Ranger – one of the state-authorized law enforcers who worked in the sparsely settled districts of Texas.

He tipped his hat to the back of his head, revealing his weather-beaten face. The first thing she had noticed about him were his eyes; steely grey, they seemed to draw her in. There was an intensity in the way he looked at her: hard, then softening as he cooed soothing words of encouragement.

His confident voice was a richly deep baritone. His complexion was rugged, burned swarthy by the glaring Texas sun. He was clean-shaven, but hadn't shaved in a while; the dark stubble on his chin and cheeks was at least three days old.

Cal brought more luggage to where she sat. One by one he lifted the containers and emptied what few items the Indians had left.

'Reckon this valise must belong to you.' He handed her a letter. It was addressed to Miss A.E. Jordan. 'Concealed in a side compartment,' he said. 'These too.' He held out more letters. 'And this money-belt, containing fifty dollars in gold pieces.'

She pushed her fingers into the first envelope and took out the letter. A small tintype picture fell into her lap.

The picture was of a young man in the dress uniform of a Union Army lieutenant, his left hand resting on a belted cavalry sabre. Hanging on to his right arm was a prettily dressed young woman: Amy Jordan, the very same girl who now held the picture in her trembling hand.

Amy read the letter, sobbing as she did so. When she had finished reading she held out the letter to the ranger and stared lovingly at the picture.

'So I am indeed Amy Jordan.' Her voice wavered with emotion. She gulped in deep breaths between loud sobs. 'I think I remember this picture.' She hiccuped. 'This is my brother.' Her tears flowed freely now.

Cal read the letter. The writing was shaky, almost childlike. It began: *Dearest Amy*, and was signed: *Your ever loving brother, Tim.* He gave his address as Fort Star, Texas.

In the letter Amy's brother described his suffering, his fears, and his fervent hope of seeing his sister, begging that she might travel to see him while he was still alive. He had contracted a mysterious illness, with symptoms like those of consumption.

Cal put down the letter with some sadness.

'Do you think he is still alive?' she asked tearfully.

The tall ranger tried hard to look away, not to betray his true feelings, but her almond eyes held his like a magnet.

'I'm sure of it,' he replied, lying. Feeling the need to change the subject, Cal told her, 'Like I say, I'll take you to Camp Sheldon. We can make arrangements for you to travel on to Fort Star when we get there.'

Amy smiled her thanks, tears flowing freely down her face; she felt suddenly so very tired, it took all her strength of will not to fall into a dead faint.

'Best get started,' he said, packing the letters into the valise, which he then tied on to his packhorse.

Cal lifted her up on to her feet. She tested her weight on the injured ankle, grimacing as she fought against showing the pain on her face.

Her hands on his shoulders, she nodded. 'I think

I will be all right. Providing you help me,' she added.

'Think you can ride?' Cal asked, repeating his earlier question.

Without waiting for her reply Cal gathered her up in his arms and carried her to where his horses waited. He set her on to the saddle of the buckskin and shortened the length of the stirrups, carefully placing her feet in them one after the other.

He turned back to fetch his canteen and noticed how his horses shuffled nervously, ears back, sensing something. The older of his two dogs snarled, teeth bared.

3

The distant report of what sounded like a gunshot echoed around the eastern foothills. Cal was alert in one swift movement. He stroked the buckskin's neck and nose.

'Easy, boy,' he cooed, drawing his Winchester from the saddle holster and an ancient telescope from his saddle-bag.

A second shot rang out; the harsh sound drifting along the valley.

Cal crossed to the stagecoach and climbed to the top of the wreckage. He raised the telescope and scanned the distant hills. Nothing alarming came into view. He moved the telescope to look along the valley, and saw what looked like a dust cloud. He focused the 'scope on that one point. It was dust all right. Dust, rising fast, the kind only made by multiple hoofs. Cal snapped the telescope shut.

The girl called out, 'What was it?' She feared the worst.

'Might be something. Might be nothing,' Cal replied. 'Best not wait around to find out.' He climbed down from the coach.

'Tell me,' she insisted.

'Riders coming. Coming fast. Best get moving.' Some unknown force compelled Cal to take another look. He threw a wooden packing-case on to the stagecoach and climbed up again, raising the 'scope to take one more look. He saw sunlight glinting on something; no Indian would be so careless as to give away his position like that. He waited a moment longer, rubbing his eyes then peering again into the lens. The dark outline of a single rider emerged through the heat haze.

Although the distance was great Cal would have sworn the rider was wearing a wide-brimmed hat. He was becoming more and more convinced that whoever was approaching was not an Indian. The sun's reflected glare dazzled Cal's eyes, clouding his vision, but he was convinced: this was no Indian.

A second rider emerged, causing Cal to look even more closely. Something red and white was fluttering in the stiff breeze; it had to be a guidon, held high above the rider's head. The ghostly white outline of a covered wagon followed close behind.

Through the dust and heat haze the outlines became clearer with every moment: blue uniforms, grey-brown mules pulling wagons. The red-and-white guidon was clear now. More riders came into view: troopers.

Cal smiled. 'Well I'll be. . . .' He remembered the girl and bit back the profanity that balanced embarrassingly on the end of his tongue.

'What is it?' she queried.

He climbed down off the stagecoach, jumping the last three feet. 'Looks like the cavalry has arrived,' he observbed. 'You'll be safe now.' Cal described in detail what he had seen. 'We'll wait for them to come up.'

He tied his coat to his Winchester and climbed up on to the coach again, waving the makeshift banner from side to side until he was sure the soldiers had seen it.

Cal watched, arm and shoulder aching, as four of the riders spurred ahead, making sure his badge was clear to see as the four cavalrymen reined in their mounts. He jumped down from the coach and strode confidently towards the newcomers, right hand raised in greeting.

'Lieutenant!' he called out. 'Good to see you.'

The leader of the cavalry party stepped down from his horse, brushing dust from his uniform. Passing the reins to a sergeant he walked forward to greet the tall lawman.

Cal extended his hand. 'Cal Avery. Texas Rangers,' he announced.

The officer saluted politely. 'Lieutenant Alvin Killeen. Sixth Cavalry. Escorting a supply column out of Fort Graham,' he announced, clicking his booted heels together smartly.

Cal was surprised to see how young the officer looked; he couldn't have been much older than twenty-one.

'What happened?' the soldier asked.

'Comanche raid,' Cal answered ruefully. 'Can't say exactly how, but my guess is that they forced the coach to swerve causing it to crash on to its side. Killed the driver, and one woman passenger. I've buried them under that juniper.' He waved an arm in the general direction of the bush. Lieutenant Killeen listened intently. 'That lucky young lady over there is the only survivor. Thing is, she has no memory of what happened. Shock, I'd say.'

He went on. 'Found a manifest that said there were eight people on the coach, including the driver and guard. No sign of the guard or the other passengers.'

'We came across two bodies on the road a ways back,' said the lieutenant. 'One was an army sergeant. From what you say the other must have been the guard.'

Cal nodded. 'Seems likely,' he agreed. 'Miss Jordan, that's the young lady there,' he pointed, 'suffered a bang on the head and a badly sprained ankle. Apart from that she seems to be OK. Except that because of the shock she's suffered she can't remember anything.'

'How did she avoid capture, and ... well, you know? asked Killeen.

'Seems likely she was thrown clear when the

coach went over,' Cal explained. 'Barely conscious when I found her in that shallow depression, hidden by the juniper.'

'May I congratulate you on a concise report, sir. Do I sense military training?'

'You do.' Cal grinned. 'Major. Army of the Confederacy during the late War between the States.' Cal said proudly.

'Cavalry?'

'Yes. Jeb Stuart's brigade.' Cal shrugged. 'That was then. Now I'm a ranger.'

'May I enquire your current rank?'

'Lieutenant, like your good self.' Cal smiled. He swivelled on his heels and led the officer to where the girl waited patiently for the men to conclude their chat.

'May I introduce Miss Amy Jordan.' The lieutenant bowed and clicked his heels together. 'Miss Jordan. This here is Lieutenant Alvin Killeen.'

Killeen removed his dusty kepi. 'Miss Jordan.'

'Lieutenant.' She held out her hand.

Killeen took it gently in his own hand, raised it to his lips, and kissed it.

The rumbling of wagons followed by the screech of wooden brakes being applied broke the mood, causing Cal to turn his head. Two covered wagons drew up in a cloud of dust. A huge bear of a moustachioed man leaped down from the seat.

'Jumbo!' Cal shouted in surprise.

'Cal Avery. Well I'll be. . . .' Jumbo Jepson wiped

his sweaty face with a red-and-white spotted hand-
kerchief. 'Ain't seen you in a coon's age. You still
ridin' for the rangers?'

The two men shook hands and clapped each
other on the back.

'Howdy, Jumbo. Yes. Out chasing Baxter Elkins
and his gang.'

'What'd they do?'

'Tried to rob the bank in Sweetwater Springs.
Come away empty. Shot two men and a woman in
that raid, plus some other people.' He frowned,
hiding the hurt inside. 'They've been selling rifles
to the Indians.'

'You find 'em?'

'Nope. Not Elkins anyways. Trail went cold on
me. There'll be another day,' he said thoughtfully.
'Got a couple of the gang, though.'

Lieutenant Killeen butted in. 'When you say you
got two of them, did you mean. . . ?'

'Sure. Two of them jumped me. Mexicans. Shot
and killed one, figure I winged the other. He high-
tailed it out of there. Been trailing him most of the
day.'

'How do you know they were Elkins's gang?'

'Fella I shot told me so before he cashed in his
chips.'

'Mexicans? This far north?'

'Surprised me as well. Old Man Elkins is recruiting from anywheres he can,' Cal said bitterly.

'Why do you call him Old Man Elkins?' the

lieutenant enquired. 'How old is he?'

Jumbo jumped in. 'Not much older than Cal here.'

'Steady on there, Jumbo,' Cal warned.

Jumbo snorted out a chortle. 'OK, he's around forty-five, give or take a year or so.'

Cal wagged a finger at his friend. 'Anyway, Lieutenant, you haven't said where you're heading?'

'Camp Bright. With two wagons of supplies.' He gestured with a wave of an arm.

'No point,' Cal told him.

Lieutenant Killeen was puzzled. 'Why?'

'Army's gone. Post's been abandoned. Moved to Fort Griffin.'

'But I have orders,' the lieutenant protested.

'No matter.' The ranger shrugged.

'You are absolutely certain?'

Cal nodded. 'Certain sure. Met a patrol three days ago. Gave me the news. They were the last troops to leave the camp. Me? I'm heading north to Camp Sheldon.'

Lieutenant Killeen looked thoughtful. 'I must consider the intelligence you have provided.'

Jumbo tapped the lieutenant's arm. 'Smoke.' He pointed to the distant hills. 'Best get movin', one way or the other.' The startled lieutenant came fast out of his reflective mood.

'Right. Gather round,' he shouted. He examined each of the expectant troopers' faces in turn.

'Change of plan, men,' he told them. 'Lieutenant Avery here has provided information that alters our destination. We will proceed to Camp Sheldon with all speed, and there await new orders.'

Sergeant Coggins, a grey-haired long-serving soldier held up a hand. 'Question, sir?'

'Proceed.'

'How far's Camp Sheldon?'

'North.' Cal answered the sergeant's question. 'About forty miles.'

Cal's keen eyes scanned the sky. Night was fast approaching. In the west the palette of yellow, orange and red streaks gave place to beautiful shades of purple. To the north and east the sky grew blacker with every minute, as angry clouds bubbled towards them.

'Storm's coming. We need to find a good spot to shelter.' Cal raised his voice above the noise of the approaching storm. 'I'll ride on ahead. Find us a place. Keep moving north, fast as you can.' Cal kicked the buckskin into a canter.

Lieutenant Killeen called back his understanding. He watched the ranger and his dogs disappear into the growing gloom, his words swallowed up by the wind.

Forks of lightning illuminated the travellers and thunderclaps crashed. Shin oak and aspen bent in the wind, sagebrush flew by, torn from the earth by the force of the wind. Over the distant peaks forked lightning lanced through black clouds. Pillars of dust, whipped vertical by fierce whirlwinds raced towards the two wagon caravan. Caps and hats pulled low, the small party struggled to make progress against the fierce elements.

Cal returned, reining in his horse alongside the lieutenant's. 'Six, seven hundred yards ahead to our right there's a deep draw with a narrow entrance. Should be wide enough to get the wagons through. Opens out a bit further on. Secure the mules in between the wagons.' His throat burned with dust as he shouted the instructions. 'Follow me.'

Lieutenant Killeen recognized that he was being given orders by a former senior officer, and relayed the order as the first drops of rain splattered on his kepi. Stronger gusts of wind whipped up everything light: leaves, small branches, and throat-clogging dust that threatened to engulf all in its path. Their hats pulled even lower over their eyes, men frantically tugged bandannas to cover their mouths and noses. In seconds gritty dust covered clothing, upon which the rain left streaks before the deluge washed the dust away.

The sky grew blacker. In an instant daylight suddenly turned to night. To answering screams of protest, teamsters and troopers urged frightened mules and horses forward, wagons bounced over rocks down a none-too gentle slope and through the narrow entrance to the high-sided draw.

Fingers chilled and raw, men desperate for

shelter hauled on ropes securing canvas. Others pulled and pushed, yanking on the reins of twisting, jerking animals that fought against being tethered, wanting only to run, scared, searching for freedom.

Under hastily erected canvas covers men huddled around spitting fires; smoky flames hissed in protest as the raw wind pelted cold, slanting rain down the draw.

The lieutenant seemed to be everywhere, checking ropes, animals and men.

Wrapped in a blanket, Miss Jordan was unceremoniously shoved under a wagon, and there she lay, motionless, alongside soldiers, heads covered, praying for salvation, hoping for the Lord's protection.

An hour or so after they had entered the draw the storm ceased with an abruptness that seemed unreal. Men, some bareheaded, checked themselves over, hands feeling for any sign of injury, fingertips massaging life back into half-frozen limbs.

Dust-streaked faces broke into broad smiles of thankfulness. The storm had passed, and they had survived Mother Nature's wrath.

Men shook hands warmly with comrades amidst peals of grim laughter and much back-slapping.

'Get those fires going again,' someone, probably Lieutenant Killeen, shouted.

Kindling was gathered; the storm had blown an abundance of twigs and branches into the draw. In no time scarlet and gold flames rose from the kindling, giving promise of warmth, illuminating the once gaunt, now much happier expressions. The welcoming aroma of coffee, bacon and beans teased empty stomachs eager for sustenance.

Against the side of one of the wagons two attentive troopers had put up a temporary lean-to for Amy. Cal squatted down next to her, a tin plate of food in his hand. He lifted a spoonful of beans into his hungry mouth, and chewed merrily.

He spoke before the food had been fully digested, involuntarily spitting out a tiny piece of bacon as he spoke.

'Sorry,' he apologized. 'Feeling OK?' he asked, brushing a hand across her sleeve.

Amy nodded and set down her empty plate. His flint-grey eyes were warm, the corners of his mouth creased with happy-lines. She had to admit that her admiration for the ranger had grown immeasurably since their meeting such a short time ago.

She smiled. 'I won't say I'm not happy to see the back of that storm.'

The firelight lit up Amy's face, highlighting the colours in her hair, enhancing the soft golden tresses framing her face. Cal allowed his eyes to take in the pleasurable sight of her. After the storm had died away Amy had washed herself and tidied her hair. Cal hadn't realized how pretty she was. Pretty was not a powerful enough word: Miss Amy Jordan was beautiful. No other word would adequately describe her.

She flashed him a quick smile, her cheeks rosy red with warmth. 'Mr Avery . . .' she hesitated briefly, then continued, 'how long have you been a Texas Ranger?'

Cal turned his face so he could look into her eyes. 'Five years,' he replied. 'When the rangers were reformed.'

'And before that?'

'Lawman, after the war,' he answered abruptly. 'The War between the States.' He clarified.

The speed and sharpness of her next question surprised him. 'Which side?'

He decided to reciprocate her directness. 'South. Jeb Stuart's First Virginia Cavalry.'

'Were you born in Texas?'

'No, miss. Virginia. I was a cadet at West Point when the war broke out.'

Amy smiled a secret smile to herself. Here was a man who outwardly gave the impression of wanting to keep to himself, but definitely wanted to talk. She asked questions about Texas. About his life in the rangers, where he lived. About Indians and rustlers. They went on talking, the time slipping away without their noticing.

Cal realized quickly that it was no good fighting against it; Amy Jordan had a way of hitting on the right question in her quest for information. Seemed like there was nothing like a pretty face to inspire a man to talk about himself.

But when it came to her turn she was not able to tell him much.

'Warm enough?' he asked.

She pulled the blanket tighter around her shoulders. 'Yes.'

For a moment there seemed nothing to say.

Cal broke the awkward silence. 'Well, I guess we'd all benefit from a little shut-eye.' He gave a slight shrug. 'I'll say goodnight then.'

'Goodnight, Mr Avery.' Her face took on a reflective look. She touched his arm. A tear threatened to form in her eye. 'Thank you again for all that you have done for me.'

He smiled. 'It was a pleasure,' he drawled. 'Anyone would have done it.'

4

Morning dawned warm and bright as a button. The rising sun streaked the eastern horizon in red, orange and yellow hues. The travellers stretched and yawned to wake up tired limbs. Men moved around without orders, knowing their jobs, fires were rekindled, weapons, equipment and animals checked and tended, coffee made, breakfast cooked.

Water still dripped from canvas covers. Horses and mules looked dishevelled and forlorn, their coats, still sodden, shining sleek in the morning sun. Troopers singled out their animals and set to work with brushes and saddle blankets to smarten up their animals' coats.

Before an hour had passed since sunup the caravan was ready to move. Cal Avery had gone at first light, his dogs trailing faithfully behind. He had gone to check out the river-crossing on the one and only trail they must take.

Lieutenant Killeen led his mounted troop along the draw at a walking pace, the gently sloping ground rising steadily to the level of the plain. All were happy to be on the move.

One hour before noon Cal Avery returned, the dust from his horse's hoofs signalling his imminent arrival. He reined in next to the lieutenant. There was no humour in his expression as he reported: 'She's just about crossable, but it won't be no cake-walk.'

Lieutenant Killeen looked back at his men, then turned his gaze back to the ranger. 'Is the river flowing deep?'

Cal nodded. 'Fast and deep. We'll need to cut logs. Attach them to the sides of the wagons. Make sure they stay afloat,' he said. 'There's a stand of cedar and pines a couple of hundred yards upstream. Should suit.' He looked at the darkening sky. 'Better pray the weather holds out.'

Killeen nodded. 'Sergeant!' he called out. Sergeant Coggins spurred his horse alongside his commander and saluted smartly.

'Take a detail to the place Lieutenant Avery will describe. Cut four good-sized trunks that can be lashed to the wagons.'

'Sir.' The sergeant returned to the troop and selected two troopers with the strongest physique. Cal dropped back to describe the place.

The first light raindrops began to fall as the sergeant's men collected saws and axes from one of the wagons, and spurred away. Amy wanted desperately to hear what was being said, and where the soldiers were going. She squirmed and fidgeted on the seat of Jumbo's wagon.

Jumbo sensed her feelings. 'Best sit still, miss. You'll find out soon enough.'

Amy felt embarrassed at Jumbo's polite admonishment; she sat still. Jumbo smiled to himself, snapping the reins to keep the mules moving. Jumbo pointed as his wagon breasted the crest of a small rise. Ahead across the plain a small herd of buffalo veered south.

Big drops of rain smacked on to the teamster's upturned face. 'Here it comes again,' he said.

'Hurry it up!' shouted the lieutenant.

Strong winds whipped the storm into every hopeful face. The storm-washed trail snaked along the bank of an arroyo. It took a good hour of struggle to reach the river.

Fifty or so feet below, the southern spur of the Brazos River, known as the Clear Fork, was a torrent of rushing red-brown water churning through the valley, the colour confirming that today the name of the river was not well deserved. Expressions changed from hope to despair as each person realized the significance of what he was looking at. As they watched, the swirling water spread wide across the land, seeming to double its width in a matter of minutes.

Jumbo reined in the team of mules and applied

the brake. 'Stay here, miss,' he ordered, climbing down from the wagon seat. He kicked a rock in front of one wheel and strode down the slope to where Lieutenant Killeen and Cal Avery sat their horses, deep in discussion. Cal turned to face his old *amigo.*

'Looks deep,' observed Jumbo, watching waves of angry water crash on to slime-covered rocks in a boiling fury.

Cal shook his head. 'Can't understand it,' he said. 'Water level's rose more than a foot in a couple of hours.'

Jumbo sighed deeply, wiping rainwater from his whiskered face. 'There's no way we're gonna get across.'

Lieutenant Killeen looked anxiously. 'Are you sure?'

Jumbo coughed and spat. 'Best find a place to get outa this storm.'

'What's your opinion?' Killeen asked Cal.

Cal leaned an arm on his saddle pommel. 'Jumbo's right. No way to cross. Current would sweep away the wagons.'

Killeen hesitated no further, 'Burke,' he called out to a trooper, 'ride upstream and tell Sergeant Coggins to bring his detail here. Tell him to forget the timber. It will be of no use.'

The sad-faced trooper rode away.

'What is it?'

The three men turned to face Amy Jordan's

question. She held a slicker over her head. She had tried hard to stay put but hadn't been able to stay patiently with the wagons as Jumbo had ordered.

Jumbo gave her a wry smile. 'River's in flood. We can't cross.'

The young woman looked from Jumbo to Killeen, then at Cal, her expression one of puzzlement.

Jumbo shrugged. 'Rainy season's started a few weeks early, miss.' He wiped his face. His voice had more than a trace of patronizing tone to it. 'No place else to cross.'

'Surely there cannot be only one suitable crossing place,' she queried unbelievingly.

Cal nodded towards the swollen river, 'This is it,' he said resignedly. 'The only crossing.'

The return of Sergeant Coggins and his detail interrupted Amy's next question.

'We going back to Fort Graham, sir?'

Lieutenant Killeen eyed the sergeant. 'Looks that way, Sergeant,' he answered ruefully, as the pounding rain began to ease a little.

'Don't surprise me,' the sergeant stated. 'Thought it was running too fast when I first seen it. I reckon a fish would struggle to get across.'

No one laughed.

Killeen spoke again, 'Sergeant, we will eat something, then get going. Dry rations only.' He took out his pocket watch, shielding it from the rain with his free hand. 'Assemble in fifteen minutes. Check animals and weapons.' He dismounted and turned to Cal, 'Mr Avery. A moment if you please.' He lifted a brown leather map case from his saddle-bag.

Cal dismounted and tethered his horse to the back of Jumbo's wagon. The two men strode a short distance away from the others. Halting at the rear of the other wagon Killeen unfastened the ties and pulled down the tailgate; he reached up and tugged the canvas cover, then spread out one of the maps, weighting down the corners with small stones.

The two men could be seen tracing imaginary lines over the thick parchment, pointing, nodding. More than once one or the other would shake his head.

Deep in thought, Lieutenant Killeen cupped one elbow in his hand, stroking his whiskered chin with his free hand whilst Cal explained some detail or other to him. Eventually Cal turned his face to look at the lieutenant; his expression was one of expectation. Killeen nodded; his loud 'yes' was audible to all. He shook Cal's hand, pushed away the stones, gathered up the map and stowed it safely in the map case.

He took out his pocket watch. 'Five minutes,' he shouted.

Cal and he accepted some beef jerky, both took a quick drink of water, then mounted their horses.

'Get them moving, Sergeant,' the lieutenant called out. 'Back the way we came.'

Cal waved his dogs on ahead as the rain ceased to fall.

As they drew near the skeleton of the stagecoach loomed out of the heat haze like a ghostly monument. Sagebrush and debris had gathered around its timber roof, blown there by the wind. Water trails snaked through the dust that covered its once bright paintwork.

Wisps of smoke rose from the hills to the south and from the direction they had travelled. Cal rode the buckskin next to Lieutenant Killeen's horse, the two men riding stirrup to stirrup, watching the horizon, chatting. The pair slowed their horses to allow Jumbo's wagon to draw level. Cal pointed.

Jumbo nodded. 'Seen 'em,' he said, flicking the reins to keep the lead mules in line. 'If you want my opinion,' he paused to look at the lieutenant, 'I'd say we should get off this road as soon as we can. We'd be better heading for Fort Griffin.'

Killeen nodded his agreement. 'Cal?' he asked the tall ranger.

Cal pushed back his hat. 'Agreed.'

Jumbo grinned, happy that his advice had been heeded. 'About four or five miles ahead there's a side trail. Used to lead to New Athens. Place is just a ghost town now. As I recall, nothing much is still standing. Anyway, a branch of it heads off north, towards the Shotton ranch. I'd say it's our best bet.'

Jumbo's bright blue eyes never left the lieutenant's face as he waited for a decision.

Killeen swatted at a fly that had landed on his cheek. 'Four or five miles it is.'

The grin on Jumbo's weather-beaten face broadened still wider as he got the mule team moving.

From the look of the uneven surface of the side trail it hadn't been used for years. Jumbo cursed loudly and frequently, apologizing to Miss Jordan each time, as he tugged and strained to manhandle the team of mules around the many obstacles nature had decided to place in his way. The muscles in his arms and shoulders bulged.

As they breasted a small rise the faint old trail dropped away sharply to a lush green valley; the freshly watered grass shone in the sunlight. Mules brayed out their protest, wooden block brakes smoked, screeching loudly, as men fought to resist the gravitational pull of the slope. Smoke turned to steam, hissing as canteens of water were emptied on to the smouldering wood.

At the foot of the slope sweating men flopped down, exhausted from their efforts. Panting animals, tongues out, sweat gleaming on their coats, stood on shaky legs, thankful for a rest.

Following the briefest of pauses Lieutenant Killeen swung the caravan north. The branch trail wound around stands of cottonwood and cedar; fortunately the surface of the track was relatively even; nothing in the rise and fall of the trail caused any difficulty.

Jumbo pointed, 'Shotton's place is just over that hill yonder.'

Lieutenant Killeen called out, 'Sergeant Coggins.

Take two men and check on the situation at the ranch. Get them to pack their essentials and join up with us. We will travel slow to allow you to catch up.'

'Sir.' The sergeant saluted, selected two of his favourites and headed off to the hill.

'If it's OK with you I'll go with them.' Cal didn't wait for the lieutenant's answer.

Killeen watched Cal and the patrol disappear over the tree-fringed crest and gave the order to proceed.

The remnants of the charred, blackened homestead stood out starkly against the verdant grassland. One or two still vertical pillars of timber marked where the cabin's walls had once stood. On a small rise the four riders sat their mounts, mouths agape as they surveyed the scene.

Sergeant Coggins was first to speak. 'Happened several days ago by the look of it.'

Satisfied that it was safe, Cal started the buckskin down the gentle slope.

'Let's take a closer look,' he said. The three soldiers followed his lead. Scavenging beasts skulked away.

A woman whom they took to be Mrs Shotton lay dead on the ground near her burned-out home. At the back of the homestead a trooper discovered the charred remains of a young girl; he took her to have been about nine years of age. The youngest of the troopers threw up. Of the man of the house there

49

was no sign.

Sergeant Coggins turned to Cal, his face a mask of sadness. 'We'll bury them. You go tell the lieutenant what we found.'

Cal grunted out his agreement and turned the buckskin back the way they had come. He caught up with the wagons and reported.

'The Shottons had two kids,' Jumbo announced. 'There was a little boy; must be three or four by now.' He blew his nose loudly.

Sergeant Coggins's detail rejoined the caravan.

Jumbo spoke up. 'Did you find a boy?'

Coggins shook his head, 'No. No sign of Shotton or a boy.'

Lieutenant Killeen broke up the unhappy conversation. 'Let's get moving,' he said. He spurred his horse forward. Cal, alongside him, said nothing; the others fell into line.

Killeen spoke, his voice a whisper. 'Seriously, how do you rate our chances?'

Cal screwed up his face; his reply was at odds with his expression: 'Good,' he answered. For a second, Cal's answer gave Killeen a warm glow in his stomach. 'As long as we can avoid the Indians,' the ranger added, stonefaced, 'and the swollen rivers.'

A gang of excited butterflies in the lieutenant's stomach leaped into action. He rode on in silence, deep in his own thoughts.

5

One hour before sunset the loud crack of a large-bore rifle echoed around the hills, followed by two more in rapid succession. The caravan halted.

'Large calibre,' Jumbo pronounced. 'Came from up there.' He pointed ahead to a heavily wooded slope.

Carbines were drawn and held ready. Eyes strained in the gloaming as the troopers waited for orders.

Moments later the tall figure of a buckskin-clad woodsman loomed out of the growing darkness; he was leading a fine-looking horse.

Jumbo called out, 'Hold your fire. That's Jack Shotton.' The teamster's keen eyes were as reliable as ever.

Lieutenant Killeen's voice rang out shrilly. 'We will make camp. Sergeant, see to the men.'

Brakes squeaked as Jumbo tugged the lever. He jumped down from the wagon and hurried forward to meet the dark figure, rubbing life back into his aching buttocks as he strode along.

The two men shook hands and talked for several minutes, the dark figure frequently waving an arm in the direction of the slope. Jumbo returned after around twenty long minutes, the woodsman and his horse had been swallowed up by the darkness.

The teamster accepted a cup of steaming coffee from a trooper.

'That was Jack Shotton,' he confirmed. 'He told me what happened.'

He related the story. 'Jack was out hunting a bear that had been troubling them. Saw black smoke and rushed home.' Jumbo blew his nose, tears welled in his creased eyes. 'He was too late to save his wife and little girl.'

He paused for breath. 'Convinced that the Indians had took his son, he went after them. Found the child on the trail, dead. Jack caught up with them and killed a couple of 'em without mercy. Told me he'd found the tracks of the rest of the war band. Said he'd be back in the mornin'.'

It was quite a story, told with every emphasis. Amy Jordan's hand never left her mouth, her blue eyes filled with terror, tears rolled down her cheeks.

A bloody Jack Shotton walked slowly into camp just as the sun rose; he made a weary silhouette against the eastern sky. The blade of the tomahawk tucked into his belt was stained with blood. Four scalps, each of lank black hair, hung from his gunbelt. His unshaven face was streaked with a mixture of sweaty dirt and dried blood.

Amy was the first to see him. She screamed at the sight of this walking ghost, not knowing if he were man or beast.

Shotton's brow was furrowed low over hooded eyes empty of emotion. Heading to the fire, he nodded a solemn silent greeting to each person he passed; every head turned, eyes followed his snail-like progress, no one was quite sure how to react to the sight of what appeared to be a dead man walking.

Jumbo and Lieutenant Killeen rose from where they squatted near the fire, neither man spoke. Jack Shotton squatted down beside them, his wild eyes raging with bloodlust.

He looked at Jumbo. 'Got a couple more of the red varmints. Still got to kill me the rest of the bunch. Stinkin' Indians.'

'Jack. You can't wipe out the entire Comanche nation single handed.'

'No Indian is safe from me after what they done to my family.' Shotton looked at the patterned sheath holding a long hunting knife on Cal's belt. 'You kill many Indians?'

'I don't hold with killing any man just for the heck of it,' Cal replied. 'Yes, I'll shoot them down like any man if they attack me. But I see no sense in killing for killing's sake. We need to talk peace and mean it. Recognize they got a right to hunt and feed their families.'

Jack Shotton scowled and turned away.

Lieutenant Killeen spoke. 'Mr Shotton, I strongly urge you to join up with us.'

The woodsman raised his eyes to look at the officer. 'Where you headed?'

'Fort Griffin.'

'You'll never make it,' Shotton said gruffly.

Before the lieutenant could make his protest, Shotton added:

'I'll go with you as far as Hancock's Creek, then you're on your own.'

'Why Hancock's Creek?'

'There's lots of Indians between here and there. I'm sick of chasin' them. Stayin' with you folks means they'll come to me.' His chilling words froze Amy's spine. 'I'll sleep over there.' Shotton gestured to a large cedar tree on the edge of the camp. He drained the tin cup he was holding and ambled away.

Daylight dawned with a chill in the air; of Jack Shotton there was no sign. After breakfast, horses were saddled, mule teams hitched up.

Cal announced that he would ride ahead to scout the area. He waved his dogs away and followed on the buckskin. Amy watched the big ranger leave, a lump of fear lodged in her throat; she felt somehow safer when he was around.

Jumbo helped her up on to the wagon seat and

whipped up the mules. He had seen the fear in her expression.

'Don't you go worryin' your pretty little head about old Cal. He knows which side his bread's buttered.' He squeezed her hand to show concern.

Two hours later Cal Avery raced the buckskin round a stand of trees, his two dogs on either side, watching his flank.

'Lieutenant. Let's shake it out a bit. You're moving too slow.'

Killeen recognized the effect but wanted to know the cause. 'What is it?'

'Indians,' Cal told him. 'Found tracks of ponies up ahead. Fifteen to twenty I'd say. Looks like they crossed the trail from the direction of the river. Headed up into those hills to the south. I can't be certain, but my guess is they're fixing to join up with a larger war party. Don't think they've got wind of us. So it's best we get up a head of speed before they spot us.'

'Any sign of Jack Shotton?' Jumbo asked.

'No. Nothing.'

Killeen gave the order, and the column broke into a canter. The wagons bounced along the trail in their wake.

'Keep the noise down as much as you can,' Cal said.

Cal pointed as they passed the pony tracks he'd told them about. About 200 yards further along the trail Jack Shotton lounged against an outcrop of rock; a stained tomahawk swung on a rawhide loop hanging from his wrist. There was one more scalp on his belt.

'Takin' your time?' He sniffed sarcastically.

Ignoring the caustic comment Cal told him about the pony tracks.

'You seen them. Me? I killed one of them.' Shotton held up a toy doll. 'He was toting this on his war belt. It was my little Jessie's. He died quiet, but *real* slow.'

The emphasis Shotton put on that one word said all there was to know about revenge.

'Can I borrow a horse?' Shotton asked. 'Mine's dead.'

Killeen nodded. 'Sergeant, cut out a horse for *Mister* Shotton.' Cal noticed the degree of contempt the lieutenant put into his words.

Amy turned up her nose and shivered at the thought of Shotton's nocturnal activities.

Jumbo let out a blast of breath. 'That Jack Shotton's one wild son of a b . . . Sorry, miss.'

'Ooh, that man. He gives me the creeps. He's like an animal.' Amy shuddered.

Jumbo patted her hand. 'You shouldn't blame him for the way he is, miss. None of us can say what we'd do if we were in his shoes.'

Amy felt ashamed to have judged the woodsman so harshly. 'Thank you, Jumbo. You are right. It was un-Christian of me.'

*

The land flattened out some, on to a wide expanse of prairie, dotted with an occasional copse of trees. Once again Cal and his dogs scouted ahead.

Red and orange streaks marbled the western sky as Cal rounded a stand of trees with some caution. The buckskin's ears had gone back, the dogs too had reacted to some unknown danger.

Six covered wagons stood side by side. Animals grazed quietly in a small clearing; oxen, a couple of cows, and two long-bearded goats.

A tall, slender man of around sixty stood and hailed Cal.

'Greetings, friend.'

Cal noticed the man's ruff under the upturned collar of his once black dust-stained frock-coat. The style of the old man's garments were from an earlier age. Cal remembered seeing such clothing in paintings back East. Under one arm he held a giant bible.

'Morning, Preacher.'

The man walked slowly towards the ranger, 'I am no preacher, friend. Although I do obey the Good Lord's teaching. We are Quakers, friend.' He waved an arm, gesturing at the group of people that had appeared from behind one of the wagons. 'My name is Weston. Josiah Weston.'

Deciding to reciprocate the man's politeness, Cal asked, 'Where are you headed, sir?'

The man shot Cal a surprised look. 'We are California bound.'

The answer surprised Cal even more so; it showed in his expression. Eyebrows raised, he said. 'You will pardon my saying so, Reverend, but this is not the regular route to California.'

'California is due west is it not, friend?'

Cal frowned. 'Yes. But. . . . It's just that I have never heard of folks travelling by way of this part of Texas before.'

'Oh.'

Cal pushed his hat off his brow. 'Do you know where you are?'

'No, friend. I fear not. I suspect we are lost, friend. Our wagon master has played us false. Colonel Key was his name. A most convincing man. He outlined the journey, and how much speedier and safer it would be to travel by way of Texas using the Royal Road, and trails known only to him, or so he claimed.'

'The *Camino Real*?' Cal could not believe anyone would be so gullible.

Josiah Weston raised his shoulders in a guilty shrug. 'It is all my fault. I should not have been so easily taken in, but . . .' he paused, 'Colonel Key gave the outward impression of being most honest and trustworthy. We . . . I,' he corrected, 'put my trust in him, and God.'

His was an old, oft-repeated story of honest people being duped by dishonest conmen who took advantage of trusting, God-fearing people.

Mr Weston continued with his story. 'Alas, all too

late we discovered the man's dishonesty, and his true intent. Once paid, he turned to drink. Three weeks into the journey we awoke to find him and several of our horses gone. Deserted without a word. We continued our journey, but somehow we appear to have lost the trail. Well . . .' he spread his hands wide, 'and as you see, friend, here we are.'

'Well, Mr Weston, you have certainly strayed a long way from the Royal Road, as you put it. You are right in the heart of Indian territory.'

'Indians, friend?' Weston was shocked.

'Yes. Indians.' Cal repeated.

'We have seen no Indians, friend. Colonel Key stated with most certainty that there were no Indians along this route.'

'Well, he was wrong, Reverend. Most certainly wrong.' Cal dismounted, 'I am a Texas Ranger.' Cal opened his canvas coat to show his badge. 'I'm with an army supply column heading for Fort Griffin. They'll be along in an hour or so. Best tag along with us. Decide what's best at the Fort.'

'No, friend, that will not do. No, it will not do at all. We are bound for California. We shall not retreat from danger.' Weston shook his head violently from side to side.

'It's your life, Reverend.' Cal shrugged. 'But if I were you I'd come to the fort with us.'

The Quaker ignored Cal's advice. 'May we offer you some refreshment, friend?'

Cal recognized blind stubbornness when he

encountered it. 'Thanks. I'll take a cup of coffee with you, if you have some.'

Weston led the way to their camp. He made the introductions and waved Cal into a fine wooden chair.

Half an hour or so later Lieutenant Killeen and his party arrived.

No amount of persuasion would deflect Josiah Western from his chosen course.

Next morning, armed with a map drawn by Lieutenant Killeen, the Quaker wagon train headed south-west, leaving behind a group of perplexed soldiers. Josiah Weston's naïve words echoed around Cal's head. He had asked what weapons the Quaker and his party carried.

'Weapons, friend? We need no weapons,' Weston had replied. 'The good Lord will protect us.'

6

Killeen's supply column hadn't been travelling for much more than an hour when a breathless teenage boy raced up on a sweating horse shouting for them to wait up.

In between gulps of air the youth explained that his father and uncle had thought through what they had been told and had decided to join them for Fort Griffin.

'Two wagons,' the boy stated, 'should be here in an hour, I guess. Pa asked, would you kindly wait for us? Please?'

Killeen gave the order to dismount, and to make some coffee. 'Might as well be civilized while we wait,' he said.

A trooper volunteered to ride back and give the boy's father the good news. Cal sensed Killeen's irritation that the two families hadn't made their decision after breakfast. He knew they were up against a dangerous time limit with threats of

Indian attack and possibly floods to contend with. However when the two wagons arrived Killeen was as courteous and gallant as Cal had seen any man.

The enlarged caravan now made slightly slower progress because of the snail-like pace of the oxen pulling the two additions. Tempers shortened considerably. Christian goodwill was strained almost to breaking point.

Evening was drawing in by the time Lieutenant Killeen called a halt for the day. The pelting rain was freezing cold, chilling bones to the marrow. The place was called Pint Creek.

Cal was surprised how well Amy Jordan was holding up; she was a strong girl, of that he had no doubt. Sadly her memory had thus far not shown much improvement despite each evening reading the letters Cal had found. A few things seemed familiar, but she could not say if it was because she actually recalled the event, or whether it was because she had just read it. It was a most perplexing time for her.

She enjoyed being the centre of attention. She was doted upon by Cal, Killeen, Jumbo, and the rest of the soldiers, who all felt very protective of her. She asked many questions, as though desperate for any information that, once learned, she could then call a memory of her own.

After supper that night Amy sat down next to Jumbo. 'Tell me a little of the rangers,' she asked. 'I heard they were formed a long time ago.'

Jumbo nodded. 'Yes, in 1823,' he reflected a moment, then made a correction. 'But they were formally constituted in 1835. They were disbanded during the war. Then, during the reconstruction, they were changed to the Texas State Police. Then again, a few years after the war ended, the Governor of Texas set about raising a new battalion of rangers. Four hundred and fifty to be precise, which he divided into six companies of seventy-five men each.' He grinned at his obvious arithmetic. 'Major John B. Jones of Corsicana, an intrepid Southern soldier if ever there was one, was commissioned to command. Anyway, the recruiting drive was successful and the rangers eventually took the field early in the spring of eighteen seventy-four. Ranger stations were located from Uvalde County in the south to Jack County in the north. There's about one hundred miles between the two main bases.'

'Were all the men Texans?'

'Heck no, miss, there's a good cross-section of nationalities, but a good number are born-and-bred Texans.'

'Was there much trouble from the Indians?'

'I'll say. Still is, as you yourself have experienced. Aside from the Comanches and Kiowas up here in the north and north-east, there's Lipans and Kickapoos in the south-west, and Chiricahua Apaches in the west.'

'Why do the Indians continue to fight?'

'They see Texas as their land, miss. A beautiful land. Wouldn't you fight for it?'

'I had never thought of it like that.'

'Mind if I join you?' Cal asked politely.

'Not at all, Cal.' Amy smiled. 'Jumbo was just telling me about the Indians.'

'Comanche Moon Raid?'

'No. Just the names of some of the tribes. What's the Moon Raid?'

'Indians live their life by the cycles of the moon. When the full moon comes they like to go raiding. Done it since ancient times. They leave the Staked Plains and thrust into Mexico to raid the big haciendas. Looking for horses and women mostly. But they'll take anything that's going.'

Amy shivered. 'Sounds horrible.'

'Nobody ever called it a picnic.' Cal shrugged.

The way the firelight seemed to shimmer in her hair warmed Cal's insides like nothing and no one else had ever done. He found more pleasure in Amy Jordan's company than he would have ever thought possible. She was pretty, intelligent, challenging, obviously well educated. She evoked thoughts and urges like no other woman he had known. He couldn't come to terms with his emotions. He had never experienced real true love, the kind described by great writers.

But Cal Avery was nothing if not a realist. In his chosen profession it wasn't helpful to contemplate the future. He harboured no illusions. There wasn't much in life as he had seen it so far to give him cause for hopefulness. He lived on the edge, living from day to day, job to job, just drifting along, doing the best he could. One day chasing murderous bank robbers, killers, rustlers. Another day fighting Indians. All had one thing in common: trouble. It seemed that in Texas trouble lurked around every bend in the trail. Maybe one day he would turn in his badge, find a good woman, settle down. Cal had to admit that the notion had some appeal. But, he reflected, could he live the quiet life, without the excitement of the chase?

His elder brother, Bart, was settled. The ranch in northern California, theoretically owned jointly, was doing OK, making a tidy profit. His brother wrote to him frequently, telling him how good life was, pleading with him to come help him work the place. Bart had qualified as a medical doctor before the war. He was married with two small children; Cal carried a tintype of them in his pocket along with one of his dead younger brother.

Over the course of the previous two days Jack Shotton had grown even more sullen and withdrawn, staying apart, shunning the company of others. At night he could be seen, a lone figure sitting cross-legged around his own personal campfire, stroking the scalps, talking to them and to the toy doll that sat facing him on a rock. When he thought someone was looking he thrust the scalps inside his buckskin shirt, turning away to mutter something quietly.

Cal had seen people go mad before. Thoughts of revenge ate away at all their sensibilities until they were transported into a distant world of their own. As far as he could recall, Shotton had not washed since the day they encountered him. The stink that pervaded the air around the homesteader was pungent and offensive. The man would have to be told soon.

The faint old trail swung more southward towards the hills, away from the sharp bend in the Clear Fork of the Brazos River through a heavily wooded deep-cut valley. Cal rode out to scout ahead, surprised and disappointed that Jack Shotton had insisted on going with him. Cal kept his distance as much as he could, pleased when Shotton decided to spur ahead.

Shotton held up a hand, momentarily halting Cal in his tracks. The homesteader dismounted and examined the soft earth. Cal nudged the buckskin alongside.

'Four ponies,' Shotton said, 'passed this way less than an hour ago.' He crept along, bent almost double. 'Walkin' slow. We can catch 'em easy.'

'Hold on, Shotton. We don't want to follow them. We need to get to the fort.'

'Uh-huh! Not me.' The homesteader leaped on to his horse and spurred away.

Cal found himself in a dilemma. What Shotton

was doing was crazy and completely opposite to what he should be doing, namely reporting what they'd seen to Lieutenant Killeen. On the other hand, his sense of human responsibility would not allow him to turn away and leave Shotton on his own.

Half a minute later he was following in the homesteader's wake.

Deeper and deeper into the gloom he rode; the dense canopy of branches and leaves suppressed much of the daylight. Up ahead the sound of two shots reverberated through the trees. Cal recognized the sound of the weapon – Shotton's large-calibre Sharps. He heard a whoop, and a cry of pain, and dug his heels into the buckskin's flanks, tugging his rifle from the saddle boot. Tree trunks flew past as the buckskin expertly veered around each obstacle. There came another whoop; another gunshot; another cry of pain.

Twenty yards ahead Shotton's horse stood motionless, its sweating grey flanks dappled by shadows. Cal saw a puff of grey smoke rise into the air, then another gunshot rang out. He guessed Shotton was behind a large boulder. Then came the pounding sound of galloping horses.

Shotton emerged from behind the boulder and raced forward. Cal stepped down from his horse and ground-tethered the animal, then heard a gurgled cry as he stepped around a large tree. Shotton turned, his hands bloody and his face a mask of crimson. His chilling laugh rang out loudly in the otherwise silent forest as he turned back to his latest victim.

The word '*No!*' caught in Cal's throat as, powerless to intervene, he watched Shotton take his gruesome trophy.

'Two more of you bastards,' the homesteader whispered, shaking the dripping blood from the scalp. He placed it carefully beside another one.

Cal saw a second dead Indian lying ten feet away.

Jack Shotton picked up his two prizes and raised himself to his full height. Then he walked slowly along the narrow game trail to where a third Indian lay panting, blood oozing from two bullet holes in his chest.

Shotton's eyes narrowed as he pointed, like an expectant child waiting to hear his parents' praise.

Cal quickened his step as Shotton reached the Indian. The long-bladed hunting knife flashed in Shotton's hand. This time the knife failed to do its grisly work.

Cal brought the carbine down hard on the back of Shotton's head.

The dying Comanche looked at Cal, a strange expression on his greying face. Then the Indian closed his eyes as his death rattle echoed through the trees.

Cal left the dead Indians where they lay. He turned Shotton over and tore the scalps from his belt, hurling them deep into the brush, as far from him as he could. He hoisted the unconscious home-steader over his horse's back, looping a rope under the horse's belly, tying Shotton's hands and feet, then led the animal to where he had left the buck-skin. He mounted and rode back to meet Killeen's caravan.

The lieutenant's eyes were wide as he listened to Cal's report. The account that he gave sickened even the hardiest of the troopers. All agreed that Shotton had gone mad.

Shotton was bound securely for his own safety, and when he started cursing and singing lewd songs he was gagged.

'We'll take the poor creature with us,' Lieutenant Killeen stated, 'and hope that someone at the fort will be able to help him.'

However, next morning Shotton had disap-peared; the ropes binding him had been chewed clean through. No horses had been taken. All that appeared to be missing was Shotton's hunting knife and his tomahawk. Both had been left overnight on the tailgate of one of the wagons. Now they were gone.

'Guess we've seen the last of him,' Jumbo observed sombrely. His relief was audible. 'Let's get going.'

On a ridge Cal Avery was seated on his horse looking at the swirling water below.

'This is where we head south,' he announced. 'We need to get across Deer Creek.'

'Or around it,' Jumbo interjected.

'We need to follow the river upstream till we find a place to cross. Maybe we'll get lucky and find Stokes's Crossing fordable. Creek narrows considerably about ten miles upstream. Usually it's not too deep at that point.'

A heavy storm came on without warning, drenching all and sundry in a matter of minutes as Lieutenant Killeen's extended caravan climbed into the foothills away from the river. Then, just as suddenly as it had started, the rain ceased, the dark sky brightened considerably and a strong wind blew away the storm. The newest members of the party were still proving to be the slowest, and straggled behind by a considerable distance, their animals being used to a more sedate pace. There was no alternative but to call a halt for a while to allow the ox-drawn wagons to catch up. Animals and humans were all in need of a rest.

Weak afternoon sunshine bathed tired faces in an eerie yellow glow as folks sat around, chatting, drinking hot coffee, speculating on the weather. The one exception was Lieutenant Killeen. He flitted around the temporary camp like a nervous bird, once or twice alighting upon a log or a rock, but unable to settle for more than a second or two.

Cal and Jumbo watched him with a mixture of amusement and sympathy. Both recognized the enormous pressure of responsibility that the young officer must feel on his shoulders.

'Coffee, Lieutenant?' Cal called out as Killeen passed near where he sat with Jumbo and Amy.

The officer turned, his eyes trancelike. 'Huh? What?'

'I asked if you want some coffee.' Cal held out a tin cup.

Killeen marched over and took the cup.

'Why don't you come sit with us a while?' Cal invited him. When the lieutenant looked likely to move on, Cal added, 'There's something I want to ask you.'

Killeen grinned nervously and accepted the seat Cal offered. 'What is it you want to ask?'

Before any answer could be forthcoming a deep rumbling assailed their ears.

'Horses,' whispered Jumbo. 'Or buffalo?' He tilted his head to one side, and nodded. 'It's horses, lots of 'em.'

Friend or foe? They could not be sure.

Cal took off his hat, grabbed his telescope and climbed up on to a rocky outcrop. The sound came ever nearer. The jingling of spurs and sabres was unmistakable to Cal's trained ear as the outline of the first blue-coated trooper came into view.

Cal jumped down from the rock and retrieved his hat.

'Cavalry,' he called out. 'Large detachment.' He turned to Lieutenant Killeen. 'Best go down to meet them.'

Killeen smiled and nodded. 'Sergeant Coggins. Guidon and standard if you please.'

Coggins and two troopers gathered up the flags, and together with Jumbo they followed Cal and the lieutenant down the slope to the trail.

7

Seeing the flags and group of men emerge from behind a stand of trees the cavalry detachment halted abruptly in a cloud of dust. Lieutenant Killeen motioned Cal and his men forward. Five blue-coated riders approached cautiously, dismounting twenty feet from Cal.

Lieutenant Killeen saluted sharply, clicking his boot heels smartly together.

'Lieutenant Alvin Killeen, sir,' he announced, adding, 'Sixth Cavalry. In command of a supply detail.'

The officer facing him returned Killeen's salute with less precision. 'Captain Chesters, Ninth Cavalry, Fort Concho. Surprised to find you here, Lieutenant.'

The two officers completed the introductions, then Killeen explained what had happened, and what he had decided and why.

Captain Chesters waved a nonchalant hand

towards his men.

'We have been chasing Lone Elk and his murderous band of combined Comanche and Kiowa tribesmen for almost two weeks. They raided homesteads and ranches north of the Colorado River. Took a number of hostages, mostly women and children. We are making a final sweep before returning to Fort Concho. Lone Elk has led us a merry dance, unfortunately proving to be very elusive. Once or twice I believed I had him, engaging in a few small skirmishes, but each time they wriggled away. The coward refuses to engage in an all-out fight. Hit and run would appear to be his only tactic.'

Cal found he couldn't keep silent. 'Lone Elk's no coward, Captain. He's feeling you out.'

Captain Chesters took an indignant tone. 'What makes you such an expert?' he snapped.

Jumbo sprang to Cal's defence. 'Years of fighting Indians. Particularly the Comanche.'

'And who might you be?' Chesters demanded.

Jumbo spat on the ground, 'I might be nobody. But the name's Jepson.' Jumbo straightened his back and puffed out his enormous chest. 'Folks mostly call me Jumbo.'

The captain looked up at the big teamster, five feet eight against six feet three.

'I can see why,' he said patronizingly. Turning away, he addressed Killeen. 'Lieutenant, I will receive your formal report in thirty minutes. Please organize a suitable place for my men to bivouac.'

Captain Chesters made to walk away, but Killeen stopped him.

'Sir. It's too early to make camp. There's still a lot of daylight left. Would it not be better to move on?'

The officer rounded on Killeen. 'I did not seek your advice, Lieutenant. However, since you have presumed to give it, I will return the compliment. My officers keep their own counsel until, and then only if, I order otherwise. Then they speak up. You will not again question my decision. Do I make myself clear?'

Killeen's throat tightened, his eyes blazed, he managed to choke out one word.

'Perfectly.' He saluted in a perfunctory manner. Chesters swung away without returning the salute, leaving Killeen, Cal and Jumbo to contemplate the latest arrival.

Cal pulled Killeen's arm. 'Best leave it for now, Lieutenant.'

The young officer was stiff with fury. 'I have never been spoken to like that. Never!' He raged.

Half an hour later, a still furious Lieutenant Killeen rapped loudly on a tent post.

'Come,' a pompous voice called out.

Alvin Killeen lifted a canvas flap, removed his forage cap and entered.

Two bright lanterns illuminated the interior of the tent. In shirtsleeves, Captain Chesters sat facing the entrance on a canvas-backed chair behind a highly polished campaign table. He was bare-headed; in his left hand he held a long thin cigar, in the right he clutched a stub of pencil. At his shoulder a hatless young lieutenant came smartly to attention.

Chesters looked at a gold pocket watch set on the table in front of him; he noted the time at the top of a single sheet of blank white paper.

'Lieutenant,' he invited.

Lieutenant Killeen delivered his formal report in a monotone, Captain Chesters's face remained expressionless throughout. His green eyes, staring directly into those of the young officer, seemed to bore deep inside the lieutenant's head. Killeen found his superior officer's intense gaze most disconcerting: his collar felt tight, his neck became damp with perspiration. He couldn't wait to get out of there.

Chesters laid down the pencil without having made one further note. He swept an unruly lock of straw-blond hair out of his eyes.

'Thank you, Lieutenant. My congratulations on a concise and excellent report.' He waved his hand in dismissal.

Killeen saluted and left the tent, unsure as to whether or not the captain's last words had been sarcastically intended. The cool evening air was pleasant and refreshing after the oppressive heat inside the tent.

Captain Chesters stubbed out his cigar and tapped his slender fingers on the table irritably. He turned his head slightly towards the man at his shoulder.

'What is your opinion of Lieutenant Killeen, John?'

The young second lieutenant moved a pace forward. 'Nervous,' he replied.

Captain Chesters selected another cigar from a leather case the young man offered.

'Think he's a coward?' he asked, accepting a light from the officer.

Second Lieutenant Dakin raised an eyebrow. He realized that nothing Chesters asked or said should surprise him, considering some of the things the captain was capable of coming out with.

'Why do you ask that, sir?'

Chesters leaned back in his chair and lifted one booted foot on to the table, blowing out a large cloud of blue smoke.

'Why else would he be so nervous?'

'Hmm?'

'I believe, John, that he is more interested in running back to the safety of Fort Griffin than doing his duty, namely fighting Indians.'

Dakin shrugged. 'We going to escort his supply column to Fort Griffin?'

The canvas chair banged down with a thump.

'Heck no! He's coming with us back to Fort Concho.'

'Can you do that?'

'John, my dear boy. You have the naivety of youth.

I have already done it. Well, in my mind I have, at any rate. I'll give him his new orders in the morning.'

Dakin frowned. 'I don't think he'll be too happy about that.'

'I don't believe I care.' Chesters grinned.

'What about the girl?'

'Keep your lustful eyes off her,' Chesters warned. 'I will look after Miss Jordan. Did you not see how she looked at me?'

Dakin was puzzled. He hadn't noticed any particular sign of encouragement from Miss Jordan concerning Captain Chesters. On the contrary, he thought her manner to have been decidedly cool.

'And the ranger? What about him?' he saked.

'He is of no account.' Chesters was adamant. 'He will do as he pleases.'

'Damn and blast his eyes!' The lieutenant threw down a piece of paper.

Cal looked across at Killeen. 'What is it?'

'*Captain Chesters's* orders,' Kileen snapped, walking away. 'Read them for yourself.'

Cal retrieved the piece of paper and read the order twice. He let out a long whistle.

'What's it say?' demanded Jumbo.

Cal's eyes narrowed as the full implications of the words hit home.

'Says you and the lieutenant are going to Fort Concho.'

'Fort Concho?' Jumbo shouted.

'That's what it says,' replied Cal.

'Fort *Concho*?' Jumbo repeated. He threw his hat on to the ground and stamped on it. '*Fort Concho*?' he yelled for a third time. 'That's crazy.'

'Seems you have no choice.'

Jumbo's already red face turned a bright scarlet.

'No choice?' he shouted. 'Like hell I ain't got no choice. My teamsters! My mules! My wagons! Where I take 'em is *my* choice.'

Amy came out of her lean-to shelter to see what the fuss was all about. Cal explained.

'But I don't want to go to Fort Concho either. I want to go with you to Fort Griffin. Where is Fort Concho, anyway?'

'More than eighty miles south of here,' Cal told her.

Amy turned to Cal. 'Are you going?'

'No,' he replied curtly.

'Well, I refuse to go too.' Amy bridled.

'That makes at least two of you,' said Jumbo wryly, picking up his battered hat. 'So you ain't fixing to go with them, are you?' he asked Cal.

Cal shook his head. 'We'll stay till we get around Deer Creek. Then I think we should head east to Fort Griffin like we planned.'

Jumbo slapped Cal on the shoulder. 'I knew you were up to somethin',' he chortled.

Troopers and wagons were strung out along the rough trail, Captain Chesters and his men in the lead.

Cal rode his horse next to Jumbo's wagon. 'Everything OK?'

Jumbo grunted. Amy put down the letter she'd been reading and smiled. She had declined Captain Chesters's offer of a horse and the chance to ride alongside him at the head of the column.

Every chance she got Amy read and reread her brother's letters.

'I feel that I am beginning to know who I am,' she had told Cal the previous night.

Each day she was able to recall events from her life. She now remembered much of her childhood and her parents.

Jumbo motioned for the ranger to come closer. 'Cal. I've been talkin' to a couple of Chesters's men. He's no Indian fighter, that's for sure. This is his first real time in the field. Only been out West six months. West Pointer.' Jumbo realized his faux pas. 'Sorry, Cal. No offence. Anyway, seems he's already lost his first lieutenant and twelve of his men, including his two Tonkawa scouts. Saw smoke and sent the lieutenant with a troop to flush 'em out while he waited in plain view. Comanches swallowed 'em up faster than you can say boo. Never came back. Found 'em all dead.' He sniffed.

'Figures.' Cal commented. 'Keep your eyes peeled. I thought I saw smoke a ways back.'

'Right.'

Cal spurred his horse alongside Lieutenant Killeen. He told him what he had seen.

'Figured I'd scout ahead a ways.' He hadn't forgotten his search for the Elkins gang.

Killeen agreed. 'Good idea,' he said.

Cal tugged the buckskin's head round and set off at right angles to the column, his dogs running along on either side.

Lieutenant Dakin called to Captain Chesters, pointing east.

'Where do you suppose he's heading?'

'Probably deserting,' the captain replied sarcastically.

Dakin cringed inwardly, but said nothing. After two weeks of campaigning he was heartily sick of his captain's constant jibes at everyone and everything. Nor had he forgiven Chesters for the naïve order that a few days ago had got his best friend killed. He watched the ranger disappear over a ridge.

8

Cal rode steadily for an hour in a wide arc over relatively flat pastureland, fording streams, keeping away from the skyline. He didn't see any smoke on any of the hills, far or near. Riding along free and easy through pretty countryside, it was easy to forget the potential dangers that might lurk at every turn. The sun on his face, a cooling breeze fanning his cheeks, these were things Cal Avery loved.

As he rode along he found his thoughts turning to the young lady he had rescued. A pretty, young *lady*, for she was that – a lady. It showed in her manners, her proud bearing, the way she spoke in that warm, velvety, sensual voice that at times was almost a whisper. He shivered at the thought of her, despite it not being cold. He still didn't know much about her, but (he smiled) he knew he liked being near her, liked being with her. Miss Amy Jordan had a way of making him feel like he was the only man around that mattered. He had to admit he'd never met a girl like her.

Her memory hadn't yet returned in full; there was still a long way to travel in that regard, but by constantly reading and rereading the letters he had retrieved she had been able to piece together much of her identity. He shrugged and smiled.

Up ahead through the trees he saw the narrow entrance to a canyon. Something about it made him pull up sharp. There was no suspicious reaction from either his horse or from the dogs. However he felt something was not right.

Ten minutes he sat, partially hidden from the canyon by a stand of shin oaks, and motionless apart from the rise and fall of his chest and the quick movement of his eyes as his gaze darted everywhere. Still he saw no movement.

Seconds later the mother dog's ears flattened against her head, her nose twitched, her top lip curled back to reveal her fangs. Cal watched as the dog's eyes looked at him, then ahead. The younger dog began to react in a similar way. Then the buckskin's ears lay back slowly.

The hairs on the back of Cal's neck bristled. Sweat formed under his arms and beaded on his forehead. Ever so slowly he shucked the Winchester out of its saddle holster and levered a round into the chamber as silently as he could. The mechanical clicks sounded like thunder in the quiet of that leafy glade.

Using only his left hand he tugged gently on the

rein to pull the buckskin's head round; the horse knew what his rider wanted and shuffled his feet to face the direction from which he had come. Cal touched his heels gently to the horse's flanks and the buckskin began to walk slowly back along the faint game trail.

Even though Cal was expecting the loud shout, when it came it made him jump. Buck whinnied and reared. Cal hung on as a wild-eyed Mexican launched his body from an overhanging branch. The horse's reaction saved Cal's life as the bandit's blade sliced through thin air. The Mexican bounced off Buck's neck, hitting the pine covered soft earth with a dull thud. An instinctive arm went up to protect his face, but too late as Buck drove his hoofs downwards with incredible force to crash on the Mexican's temple.

Cal dug in his spurs, and Buck shot forward into a gallop, leaving behind more war-whooping. Gunshots rang out and the bullets flew past Cal's ears. He didn't look back, but kept his eyes firmly fixed on the trail in front of him. On his left two more bandits ran towards him, their faces gleaming with sweat. One was taking careful aim with a rifle, the other pointed a six-gun. Cal let go the reins and raised the Winchester, firing off two shots in rapid succession. Both bandits dropped like a stone, hit dead centre by the ranger's bullets.

Up ahead a pinto pony emerged from the brush. Cal took deadly aim and a fourth bushwhacker bit the dust as he sped past. Crouching low and controlling Buck's direction with his knees, Cal let the horse have his head, confident that the big horse knew what was expected of him. Cal knew Buck wouldn't let him down.

Behind him Cal heard the pounding of hoofs. He raised the rifle and turned in the saddle, expecting to shoot his pursuer, but saw only the riderless pinto pony.

Twenty minutes later, satisfied he wasn't being followed, he slowed Buck to a canter, then to a walk. Trees were sparser now, open ground lay ahead. Cal stopped in a small copse of cedars and listened intensely. The only sounds were the breeze stirring the leaves in the trees, the panting of his horse and dogs, and the pounding of his own heart. He couldn't be sure of the identity of the ambushers, but decided against going back to find out.

'Maybe they were part of the Elkins gang,' he said to Buck, and received an answering snort.

He dismounted, watered and fed Buck, then reloaded the Winchester, pleased to have escaped the ambush without a scratch.

Half an hour later Cal stepped up into the saddle.

'Come on, horse,' he said. 'Let's get back to the column.'

Seeing no sign of Indians, an impatient Captain Chesters weighed up the situation.

'Lieutenant Killeen. Take your fifteen men and

sweep south-east of the river. Find a way to force the Comanche and Kiowas north. I'll take the rest of the men and swing north-west. We might catch old Lone Elk in a pincer movement.'

Killeen frowned, 'I wouldn't bank on it, Captain. From what Cal Avery said, Lone Elk is one crafty Indian.'

Chesters flashed the lieutenant a look designed to turn salt to stone. He turned away.

'You have your orders, Lieutenant,' he said. He added with a grunt. 'As you seem to be so concerned, if you can find that ranger you had better take him with you.'

Night was fast approaching when Killeen's troop eventually crossed an Indian trail. He and Sergeant Coggins dismounted to get a closer look at the tracks.

'Looks to be at least thirty of them. Heading west,' opined the lieutenant.

Corporal Bob Gates, an old army scout, leaned across his horse's neck and nodded. 'Sure looks that way.'

Sergeant Coggins urged his horse alongside Lieutenant Killeen's. 'Men are tuckered out, sir. Reckon we should make camp. There's good water and shelter up ahead.'

Killeen nodded. 'OK, Sergeant. Lead the way.'

The sergeant led the weary troopers along the narrow trail and down a gentle slope to where a fast-flowing stream gurgled through rocks.

'Dismount,' ordered Coggins. 'See to your animals.' He turned to a young trooper, 'O'Hara, get a fire going.'

On a sharp bluff high above, dark eyes watched the soldiers set up camp. In the shadow of the trees the war-band leader sighed with relief. For a while he had been convinced that the soldiers would catch up with them. The Indians were painted for war, but even if they made a surprise attack, at two to one the odds favoured the cavalrymen. Now the soldiers had made camp almost within gunshot of their position. He motioned to the three braves at his side to slide away from the edge of the escarpment. Four now became eight as the two halves of his band joined together.

Silently the Indians walked their ponies across a narrow ridge, along an old game trail, brushing out foot and hoofprints with branches cut from fir trees, not intending to stop until they were at least three hours away.

The morning dawned drab and drear. Rain had fallen during the night, soaking bedrolls and clothing. Even using their slickers for an over-blanket the soldiers had spent an uncomfortable night.

Drops of rain still dripped from leaves bent low by the deluge as Sergeant Coggins ambled over to where the lieutenant was sitting.

'I sent Bob Gates out a coupla times during the night, sir,' he said. 'Didn't see much. Rain's washed away the tracks we found yesterday.'

Killeen shrugged. 'Figured as much.'

'We gonna follow the river, Lieutenant? Beggin'
your pardon for askin',' a nearby trooper asked.

Killeen looked at Sergeant Coggins for reassurance. The sergeant nodded.

'Yes, Trooper,' Killeen said. 'Downstream.
Sergeant, you take half the troop and move along
half a mile or so from the river. I'll take the others
along the riverbank. If either of us finds tracks, he
is to send for the other. Two shots in rapid succession means come fast. OK? I'll take Corporal Gates
with me. And Sergeant. No independent action,
understood?'

Sergeant Coggins saluted and went to organize
his men.

Half an hour later a thunderstorm came on
without warning. Their slickers gleaming with water,
Lieutenant Killeen led his half of the troop through
a slide of mud on the riverbank. The tracks of
several unshod ponies stood out clearly, small pools
of rainwater gathering in the indentations.

'Fresh tracks,' whispered Gates. 'Must be close
by.'

Killeen turned in the saddle. 'Pass the word, keep
your eyes peeled.'

Sergeant Coggins and his men stood in a glade of
cedar trees at the side of the trail 500 yards further
on. Lieutenant Killeen held up a hand to halt his
men.

The cavalryman reported that they hadn't come across any sign of Indians.

With darkness fast approaching, Lieutenant Killeen decided to make for the rendezvous point.

Captain Chesters eyed the approaching dust cloud apprehensively.

'Three white men pursued by a group of hostiles.' Lieutenant Dakin observed. He turned, slotting his binoculars into their case.

Chesters raised a gauntleted hand to halt the column. 'First two squads, skirmish line.'

The troopers grabbed carbines, dismounted in an orderly fashion and deployed across the front of the column with impressive, well-drilled precision.

The three riders galloped through the line of kneeling soldiers, halting when they reached Captain Chesters, their horses white with lather. One man was bareheaded, blood ran down his face.

Chesters's voice rang out clear and confidently. 'Fire at will.'

Two of the pursuing Indians went down, the other five or six turned their ponies and sped off.

'Much obliged, General. Appreciate it,' said one of the white riders.

'It's Captain. Captain Chesters. And you are?' queried Chesters as the men recovered their breath.

'Jake Elkins. This is my brother Kyle. That's my nephew, Jared.' The newcomer dug out a sheaf of papers from inside his coat and held them towards the officer.

'My credentials.' He nodded curtly. 'I am acting deputy US marshal, and the Indian agent for this part of Texas.'

Chesters response was cutting. 'Judging by the send-off you have just received, it would appear that you are not the Indians' favourite agent by any means.'

Jumbo stood on the wagon seat to see what was happening.

'By God, I'm certain that's Jake Elkins,' he said to Amy. 'Cal ain't gonna like seein' him here.'

'Why?'

'Cal hates his guts,' Jumbo explained. 'Figures Jake's in league with the ones Cal's been trailin', namely his cousin, Bax Elkins, and his gang.'

'And are they?'

Jumbo scratched a tick out of his moustache. 'Cal thinks so. Reckons Jake's the big gun.'

'Where are you and your men headed, Captain?' Elkins asked.

'Fort Concho.'

'Oh.'

'Why do you react so?'

'Nothing. Just that I suppose I guessed you'd be headed for Fort Griffin as it's nearer. I have agency business in The Flat.'

Captain Chesters had heard about the lawless settlement that had sprung up around Fort Griffin called The Flat. A town full of buffalo hunters, cow-punchers, gamblers and whores, frequented by soldiers from the fort. As explosive a mixture as could be found on the frontier. He surmised that discipline must be extremely lax at Fort Griffin. No way would he allow any of his men to frequent such a notorious den of iniquity.

'No,' Chesters said emphatically. 'We are bound for Fort Concho.'

Intrigued, Jumbo had made his way to the head of the column. Elkins recognized him. He nodded a greeting.

'Jepson.'

Jumbo ignored the greeting. He grasped the bridle of Chesters's horse.

'Cap'n, this man is part of the gang Cal Avery is looking for.'

Elkins started on hearing the name.

'Avery?' he queried. 'Huh? What you say? That no-good skunk is looking for *me*?' Elkins snarled. 'You got it all wrong, Jumbo. The law's after Avery. Namely me. I got a warrant for his arrest.'

Jumbo bristled. 'What for?'

'Murder!'

The word excited ripples of curiosity through those who heard it.

'Avery made no mention of this,' Captain Chesters said angrily.

'He's here?'

Lieutenant Dakin butted in. 'Out scouting.'

'Captain. Four weeks ago Avery gunned down two men in The Flat. Shot them in the back.'

Jumbo sprang to his friend's defence. 'Cal's a Texas Ranger. He never backshot anybody.'

Elkins appeared unswayed. 'Marshal Hines handed me the warrant himself. And in any case the rangers have suspended Avery,' he said coolly.

'He's a liar,' Jumbo yelled. 'Don't believe him.'

'Did he tell you he was unofficial?'

Captain Chesters stared at Elkins. 'What do you mean, unofficial?'

'Avery's off the reservation.' Elkins grinned. 'He's acting alone. Savvy? He has no legal standing.'

'I understand you perfectly well, Mr Elkins,' said Chesters sharply.

Ominous dark clouds threatened to engulf the land. Over the distant hills the sky crackled with thunder. Heads turned to face the sound of hoofs, as the air grew heavy, the freshening breeze whipping guidons and flags into a brisk dance.

Cal Avery rode in. Jumbo raised a hand in greeting, hoping to warn his friend. The conversations of others stilled as all watched the the approach of the big ranger.

When Cal saw who was sitting his horse next to Captain Chesters, his expression grew furious, his face reddened as he felt the anger rise from the pit of his stomach.

He pointed at Jake Elkins. 'What's he doing here?'

Lieutenant Dakin was the first to speak. 'Mr Elkins is the Indian Agent.'

Cal laughed loudly. 'He's what?'

Captain Chesters felt that as commanding officer it was beholden upon him to provide the answer.

'His papers are bona fide. I have checked them myself.'

'You've got to be kidding. He's no Indian agent.' Cal glowered. There was no humour in his response. 'He's nothing but a tinhorn gangster.'

Elkins screwed up his face. 'Captain. I resent that remark,' he said, feigning indignation. He turned to Cal. 'What you don't know, Avery, is that I'm a bona fide US marshal.'

'Acting deputy,' shouted Jumbo.

Elkins ignored the big teamster. He waved a sheaf of papers. 'This here's a warrant for your arrest.'

'On what charge?' Cal demanded heatedly.

'Murder.'

Captain Chesters interrupted. 'According to Mr Elkins you have been suspended from active duty. Is that correct?'

Cal looked from one face to another, his own was racked with frustration. For the briefest of moments he was torn between telling the truth and committing an act of murder. His eyes blazed with fury; he wanted nothing more than to squeeze the life out of Elkins's neck. He pushed back his coat to reveal the butt of his six-gun, then he released the rawhide thong off the hammer in one slow deliberate movement.

Chesters guessed Cal's intention and was having none of it.

'Stay your hand, Avery,' he called out. His tone was commanding. 'Sergeant, cover this man.'

Carbines were drawn from saddle boots, shells clicked home with mechanical precision. Cal found himself looking down the barrels of five or six rifles.

Captain Chesters urged his mount close to the ranger's.

'I will have no gun play here. Your behaviour confirms Mr Elkins's assertion that you are prone to violence. He tells me he has tried to reason with you on more than one occasion, but you refuse to hear him out.'

'He's a liar.'

Kyle Elkins spoke for the first time. 'Captain, my brother fears for his life.'

'And well he might,' said Cal. 'My kid brother was one of the two men he and his gang gunned down. I'll kill him first chance I get.'

Chesters held out a hand. 'I will have your gun, if you please.'

'You will not, sir.' Cal's eyes narrowed. 'I do not please.'

Chesters nodded to the sergeant. He and one of the troopers rode to come alongside Cal's horse, one either side.

Chesters repeated. 'Your weapon, sir.'

'No!'

Cal's defiant refusal drew a shout from Amy, who

had joined the party at the head of the column. 'No, Cal, don't.'

The ranger glanced sideways. Amy was shaking her head from side to side.

'No,' she repeated.

Cal lifted the six-gun from its holster and held it, butt forward, to Captain Chesters.

'I am glad you have shown some sense,' Chesters said, tucking the gun into his belt. 'In view of these developments I have no choice but to place you under arrest.'

Cal said nothing.

'Do I have your word that you will not try to escape?'

'You have it.'

'Lieutenant Dakin, until such time as Lieutenant Killeen sees fit to return, you will take charge of the prisoner.'

Jake Elkins couldn't resist the opportunity for a snide comment. 'By the way, Avery, how's your kid brother?'

The sergeant and the trooper grabbed Cal's arms before he could get at Jake Elkins. All Cal wanted to do was to rip the man's head from his shoulders.

Elkins was determined to continue with his tormenting. He looked at Chesters. 'Kid tried to gun me down. Luckily I got a shot off.' He snarled. 'Dead, is he?'

9

Lieutenant Killeen and his men were waiting at the rendezvous point. Chesters apprised him of what had happened and placed a disgruntled Cal Avery in his charge.

Captain Chesters led his blue-coated column along a valley trail that wound between sage-covered hills. Gritty dust clung to skin and clothing. Behind the column wagons rumbled and jostled along the stone-littered track. Nervous troopers peered into the heat haze for any sign of Indians. Lieutenant Dakin looked across at his commander.

'Do you think we've lost them, sir?'

'I hope not, John. I sincerely hope not.'

Despite the captain's confident tone the young second lieutenant recognized concern in his commander's voice.

Further back along the column, Cal Avery sat his horse with strained patience. Alongside him, his newly acquired friend, Lieutenant Killeen, rode stoically, his jaw set firm in frustration.

Not so long ago he had been in command of his own supply detail; his first real command. He had loved the freedom of being able to use his own judgement: to make his own decisions. Now he was forced by military etiquette to serve an officer whom he believed to be incompetent: a man with little or no experience of frontier soldiering. It was an intolerable situation and he loathed it with a vengeance. He had never before resented a senior officer, or balked at any order, not until now. Captain Chesters had changed all that.

Killeen looked around, past the fifteen troopers that made up his command, to the leading wagon of his original supply column. Jumbo Jepson flicked the reins to keep his mule team in check; beside him sat the beautiful and delectable Miss Amy Jordan. Alvin Killeen pined for her. The ache in his heart was even greater than his hatred of Captain Chesters. He sighed deeply and longingly.

So far Amy Jordan had shown him polite courtesy and friendship, but nothing more. If anything she appeared to have given her favours to the big Texas Ranger; and who could blame her, Killeen thought. Cal Avery was a tall and powerful man with a commanding presence. Handsome in a rugged way. Seemingly unflappable. Honest and trustworthy. A man of the law, not a man against the law as that man Elkins claimed.

Killeen liked the ranger, delighted in his company. Trusted his judgement. Yes, his rival was everything any man would aspire to be.

Amy gasped, startling Jumbo who almost dropped the reins.

'What is it?' he asked,

She held up a letter. 'It's all coming back to me.'

Jumbo tried to focus on the letter and on the track at the same time. 'What is?'

Her eyes were wide with excitement. 'My parents died when my brother and I were very young. We were raised by our maiden aunt, Father's sister, childless, she was our only living relative. I remember now. She was strict. We hated her.' She waved the letter. 'We formed a strong bond, my brother Tim and I; us against the world, but mostly against Aunt Harriet.'

She planted a kiss on Jumbo's whiskered cheek. 'Isn't it wonderful, Jumbo? I can remember.'

'Sure are happy for you, miss.'

Amy looked across at Cal, intending to share her returned memories with the ranger. He aroused her curiosity. He seemed to be a well-educated and gentle man who, for some reason that she had not so far been able to wheedle out of him, loved being a Texas Ranger, and favoured life on the open range. He appeared to revel in the dangers to be easily found there. She found herself increasingly drawn to him, loving his company. She blushed at thoughts that entered her head when she considered her feelings for him: a strange, compelling attraction, like nothing she had ever experienced.

The look of thunder on the ranger's face told her now was not the time to intrude upon his thoughts.

The brooding Cal Avery could hear Jake and Kyle Elkins up at the head of the column joking with Captain Chesters and that sick puppy of his, Lieutenant Dakin. Their laughter, although not loud, assailed Cal's ears. Only Lieutenant Killeen's timely intervention had prevented Chesters having the ranger's hands tied.

It was bad enough that they had taken his weapons, but how could those two officers be so taken in by that skunk Elkins? To have taken his word against that of a Texas Ranger lieutenant was unbelievable. Captain Chesters had sure been impressed by Jake Elkins's official government position. Cal knew that Elkins had bribed and blackmailed his way to the job.

'Every dog will have his day,' Cal said softly.

'What?' enquired Alvin Killeen.

'Nothing.'

Cal knew that sooner or later Lone Elk would lead his enlarged band of Comanches and Kiowas against Captain Chesters's small force. The cavalry would be outnumbered. Heading south-west across the parched flatlands was not the way to go. Chesters's column couldn't hope to outrun the Indians, and out there on the prairie there would be no cover. South towards the hills was the way, where there was plenty of good cover, trees, rocks, ravines and deep washes, where they could hide or find a place adequate to present a robust defence. Cal estimated that in another hour or so it would be too late; they would be out on the prairie, exposed, vulnerable to attack.

'I know what you're thinking.' Lieutenant Killeen's voice brought Cal out of his doleful reverie.

'Yes?' he queried.

Killeen nodded. 'I reckon you think we should be heading south, or better still south-east.'

Cal smiled thinly. 'Am I that obvious?'

'Uh-huh,' Killeen replied prudently. 'Cal, if things look bad, I hope you know you can count on me.'

Cal smiled an unspoken thanks.

'There's a Colt .45 in my saddle-bag,' Killeen went on, 'and a box of cartridges.'

Cal patted the lieutenant's arm. 'Thanks,' he said.

Twenty minutes later Cal Avery touched Lieutenant Killeen's arm again.

'Alvin. You have somehow to persuade Chesters to change direction. There's a deep draw back about half a mile. Sides banked up like a fortress. We should hole up there tonight.'

Killeen looked into the ranger's gaunt face.

Cal continued, 'There's Indian sign all over the place. Reckon they'll hit us in less than an hour. If we don't turn back soon, it'll be too late.'

Corporal Gates was riding close behind the two

men. He spurred his horse forward.

'Begging your pardon, Lieutenant, but Cal's right. They might even attack before then.'

Lieutenant Killeen nodded; he knew what he had to do. He dug a hand inside his saddle-bag and came up with a six-gun. He handed it to Cal, then delved into the saddle-bag again, fetching out a box of cartridges.

'There's a spare Winchester under the seat in Jumbo's wagon,' he told Cal. 'Sergeant Coggins.' he called out, 'guidon. Gates, you come too. Follow me.'

The three cavalrymen kicked their mounts into a fast canter, disappearing in a cloud of chalky dust.

Lieutenant Killeen rode his detail in front of the column, and turned to face the blue-coated officers at the front. He held up a hand.

Captain Chesters, not knowing what was going on, did the same, bringing the column to a stuttering halt.

'What is the meaning of this, Lieutenant?' he challenged.

Lieutenant Killeen explained his reason for halting the column, introducing Corporal Gates and calling on the ex-scout to add his own opinion and recommendation. Killeen was faced with a flat rejection of his advice from Captain Chesters.

'Nonsense!' snarled Chesters irritably.

Killeen tried to protest, but Chesters stayed him

with a hand.

'I hear what you say, Lieutenant, but you are wrong.' He gestured with an arm across the prairie stretching out in front of him.

'Look,' he said, his tone that of a patronizing parent. 'See for yourself. The Indians have gone. They have recognized the presence of a well-trained and superior force and have gone back to their tepees and squaws.'

Lieutenant Killeen was unmoved by the captain's remarks.

'No sir,' he said adamantly. 'It is you who are wrong. I refuse to lead my men into a trap.'

Captain Chesters's false smile failed to mask the sarcasm in his voice. 'Then, Lieutenant, you shall have your wish.'

Killeen fought back a smile of triumph. However, any spark of pleasure he felt was quickly extinguished by Captain Chesters's follow-up.

'Lieutenant Killeen. I hereby relieve you of your command. Lieutenant Dakin will assume your duties.' Chesters's raised hand silenced Killeen's protest. 'Consider yourself under arrest. I intend to have you court martialled for cowardice.'

For a moment Lieutenant Killeen was dumb-struck.

'Sergeant!' yelled Captain Chesters, 'escort your ex-commanding officer back to his place in the column. Killeen, for now you may keep your sword. Dismiss.'

Sergeant Coggins turned to the open-mouthed lieutenant.

'Best get back, sir.'

Lieutenant Killeen allowed the sergeant to guide his horse back to his men. Lieutenant Dakin followed at a suitable distance.

Once back in line Killeen told Cal what had happened.

'Chesters is a fool,' was all the ranger said.

At that moment about fifteen whooping Indians appeared from the depths of a shallow arroyo 300 yards to Captain Chesters's right. A warrior fired a single shot at the soldiers, then turned and sped away.

Cal and Killeen heard Chesters's shouted order.

'First four squads, get those Indians. Follow me. Bugler, sound the charge.'

Cal shouted, 'No!' But it was no use.

Captain Chesters and the troopers spurred away in pursuit of the Indians.

'It's a trap,' Cal shouted at the top of his voice. 'He's leading them into a trap.'

'We must support him,' Lieutenant Dakin urged.

'Too late,' Cal called out ruefully, 'Alvin, you must take command. Get us back to that deep draw. Fast as you can.'

Lieutenant Dakin piped up. 'I protest most strongly. I am in command. Lieutenant Killeen is under arrest.'

'Oh shut up,' Killeen told him. 'Column,' he

shouted, 'right wheel. Back to that draw.'

Cal was back with the wagon. He told the two Quaker families to cut their oxen loose and to abandon their wagons.

'Climb into Jumbo's and the other wagon. We'll come back for your things later.'

His passengers aboard, Jumbo slapped the reins on the backs of the mules and raced back along the bumpy trail.

Even before they were halfway to the draw, the sound of heavy fighting could be heard. Forty or fifty Indians appeared on a small crest about 800 yards away. Troopers bent low over their horses' necks, digging in spurs, slapping flanks, shouting words of encouragement, as the Indians began to charge.

The fast-moving column was swallowed up in the deep draw.

'Skirmish line,' shouted Lieutenant Killeen.

'Get those wagons into an arrowhead, horses and mules in the centre,' Cal yelled. 'Barricade the open side with anything you can find.' He caught the Winchester that Jumbo threw to him as he leaped from Buck's back. 'Fire at their ponies.'

Women and children screamed as the first shots rang out. Jumbo helped Amy down from the wagon and rushed to join Cal.

A number of Indians went down in the first wave. In the distance a bugle sounded the charge. In the draw every member of the column prayed for the safe deliverance of Captain Chesters and his men.

The Comanches charged again. This time ten ponies went down and two or three Indians stayed down. Others got to their feet and ran out of range. A mist of grey, acrid gunsmoke filled the draw as the troopers maintained their rate of fire.

Less than a mile away Captain Chesters led his men into the ambush that Cal had predicted. The band of Indians he was intent on pursuing turned their ponies to face the cavalry charge. From the right and left other bands of Comanches and Kiowas drove at the soldiers.

Captain Chesters shrill voice pierced the air.

'Fire at will. Sabres. Charge.'

Swords and tomahawks flashed as the two forces locked in a mêlée of fighting.

'To me. Form on me,' Chesters shouted.

The ringing sound of steel upon steel echoed across the plains; shot after shot rang out as on both sides men fought for their lives. Chesters tore off the end of an arrow that embedded itself in his shoulder, the trooper closest to him was almost decapitated by a huge Comanche, whom Chesters shot through the temple.

In the dust-saturated atmosphere it was difficult to see clearly. A corporal bellowed a war cry as he cut down two braves with a thrust and backslash of his razor-sharp sabre before he was overwhelmed by four Indians, his dying screams piercing the air.

Chesters hung on desperately to his horse when a tomahawk caught him a glancing blow on the arm. His kepi gone, he still barked out orders, blood and sweat mixed with burnt gunpowder streaking his face.

Miraculously the bugler at his side remained unscathed.

'Sound recall,' Chesters panted, dismounting.

The bugler licked his parched lips and blew, but for a split second no notes sounded.

'Sound recall,' yelled Chesters. 'To me, to me,' he shouted as a Comanche brave knocked him to the ground.

Sergeant Walters speared the Indian with his sabre and helped his captain to his feet as other troopers fought their way to where the troop guidon flapped briskly in the strong breeze. The sergeant added his voice to shouts of, 'At 'em, men!' arms and shoulders aching with pain.

Five or six still-mounted troopers appeared on the left flank, desperately urging their frightened horses towards the flags, firing pistols. Sunlight glinted on flashing sabres, gun flashes seemed bright in contrast with blue coats.

Bullets whined, arrows flew, sabres, tomahawks and knives cut through the greying air as individuals fought their own battle to hold on to their lives.

A group of Comanches leaped forward, fresh to the fight, threading their way over heaped bodies of dead and wounded soldiers and Indians. Every

trooper knew that there could be no thought of sur-
render; to do so would mean being cut down
viciously. This was a life and death struggle, produc-
ing sights of such carnage a would sicken any citizen
to the pit of his stomach.

Just when the Indians were beginning to sense
victory Captain Chesters and his men redoubled
their efforts, somehow finding hidden depths of
courage and strength.

During a short lull Captain Chesters leaned on
his sword; his hands shook visibly as he reloaded his
pistol. A tiny hiss of steam rose from the hot barrel
as a drop of sweat fell from his brow. Chesters wiped
his sleeve across his forehead, then shot an onrushing Indian.

He noticed the bugler at his side, the young
man's face set in a determined grimace, his eyes
seemed to plead with his commander to do something to save him. Chesters felt the guilt of
command for leading his men into a trap. His
intense pride and sense of duty would not allow him
to permit these savages to beat him and his men
into submission.

'Sound recall,' he cried.

The bugle sounded loud and clear, a rallying call
above the ranks of whooping Comanches. The
bugle's sound seemed abruptly to stall their
advance, as well as giving fresh impetus to the cavalrymen.

A bloodied Sergeant Walters stood back to back

with other troopers, shielding Captain Chesters and a group of wounded men. One trooper struggled to keep hold of the reins of the spooked cavalry horses that shied, snorted and reared, wanting only to flee the blood-soaked scene. Walters remembered his injured forearm, forgotten during the fierce fighting, when it had seemed numb. Now that he focused his attention on it, stinging pains shot up his arm. His sleeve was soaked in blood, and he thought again how strange that blood looked black in the shadowed gloom of the fighting. He rolled up the sodden sleeve; fumbling for a kerchief to wrap around the already bruised wound, pulling the cloth as tight as he could, holding one end in his teeth, as he held off a tomahawk-swinging Comanche with his sabre.

Beside him, Corporal Gates fired his pistol at point-blank range into the face of an enemy; Walters noticed that the front of Gates's uniform was streaked with blood. Gates saw the look.

'Hope it's not mine, Sarge.'

Walters nodded his head in the direction of the screams of wounded men.

'Captain,' he said to Chesters, 'We need to try to get away.'

Captain Chesters knew the sergeant was right. He also knew that this battle wasn't over by a long shot. A voice in the back of his head told him it was still winnable.

'We need to get back to the column,' urged

Sergeant Walters, looking deep into his captain's proud eyes. He realized that this officer would never give the order to retreat, but this was suicide. This served no purpose. The Indians outnumbered the cavalrymen by more than three to one. There was no hope of victory. *Death or glory*. He recalled the words shouted by his colonel during the Civil War. Crazy officers. Walters and three others had been all who survived that suicidal frontal assault on a Confederate position. '*There's a time to die, and a time to live to fight another day,*' he said softly under his breath.

Captain Chesters slumped to the ground, knocked unconscious by a whirling war-club. Sergeant Walters knew he had to act fast; there was no time to lose.

'Bugler. Sound recall, then retreat.' He grabbed the reins of a horse. 'Mount if you can. Come on, follow me.' He reached down from the saddle. 'Help me with the captain,' he told a trooper. Around him other men were mounting. Horses kicked hoofs at the massed ranks of Indians, and somehow the group of cavalrymen were on horseback, slashing down glinting blades of sabres. Pulling men up behind them as they rode, they swung carbines at the enemy when their ammunition was gone.

'Sound the charge,' Walters yelled, and the big horses forced a path through the hostiles. To the bugler, who was sitting behind a trooper and holding on for dear life, he shouted, 'Keep blowing that thing, boy.'

Suddenly, led by Sergeant Walters who had one wounded arm around the slumped body of his commanding officer, the group of horses emerged from the crowd of milling Indians. Heads low, backs bent over the necks of their mounts, the soldiers dodged bullets and arrows that were fired after them. One screaming horse went down, spilling its two riders to the ground; seconds later their bleeding bodies were pounced upon by a group of Indians.

The native warriors swarmed after the remaining cavalrymen, rifles belching leaden death, bullets kicking up bursts of sandy earth as they fell, spent, to the ground all around them.

Corporal Gates felt the wind of an Indian bullet whip past his cheek, plucking at his coat-collar as it passed. And suddenly they were clear.

10

On the banked-up earth above the side of the draw, Lieutenant Killeen and the rest of the column fired fusillade after lethal fusillade into the Indians who were charging with carbines and pistols. In the confused smoke-charged atmosphere one or two Indians made it past the troopers' steady rate of fire.

More and more Indians managed to beat the fusillade of shots to break through the skirmish lines of the soldiers, leaping their horses over the natural rampart. Not realizing that a sheer drop lay on the other side, many of the ponies making the jump broke legs in the fall that followed, their native riders being met with a merciless response from the desperate defenders, who dispatched them with unsympathetic blows from rifle butts and thrusts from sabres.

Cal parried a swinging tomahawk, then side-stepped to ram the barrel of his Colt into the Indian's mouth, finishing the man off with his

Bowie knife.

The sound of a bugle call echoed around the fighting men as the remnants of Captain Chesters's four squads galloped into the draw, their uniforms streaked with blood, theirs and their enemy's. They dismounted at the run, some with carbines clutched in their hands, some with bloodied sabres, others with six-guns, calling for ammunition.

The newly returned troopers swelled the ranks of the defenders. Sergeant Walters, his bloodstained uniform tunic almost ripped from his back, rode in with a hatless and barely conscious Captain Chesters clinging to his waist. A trooper caught hold of the bridle, careful to avoid the ferocious bite of the big sorrel: the war horse's eyes were wild with terror. A Quaker man ran over to support the captain while his wife helped lower the officer to the ground. Blood trickled down his face from a wound on his temple; the stub of the broken off arrow in his shoulder was hidden by his stained yellow bandanna.

Chesters managed a weak smile of thanks. The troop's medical orderly, Henrik Schmidt, found a bottle of spirits and gave the officer a slug. Blood dripped from the fingers on Chesters's left hand. He coughed up a mouthful of crud, then sat up without assistance. Chesters saw where the orderly's eyes were looking. Schmidt pointed to the arrow shaft.

'Say nothing,' Chesters said. The orderly nodded.

'My thanks to you, Schmidt,' Chesters held out his right hand. 'Help me up, please.'

Orderly Schmidt did as his commander requested. Chesters limped away, reloading his service revolver.

Schmidt took off his glasses and wiped them on his sleeve. He had never seen anything like it. A man with multiple wounds intent on continuing the fight, when by all known medical laws they should be digging a hole to bury him in.

'That's one strong man,' Schmidt said out loud.

Captain Chesters appeared at Cal's shoulder. The ranger paused from firing his Winchester, not believing his eyes.

Schmidt ran up and attempted to wrap a bandage around the captain's gaping head wound. Captain Chesters stood still for only a moment.

'Hurry up, man,' he said impatiently.

Schmidt pinned the bandage and ambled away to treat other wounds, pleased to have satisfied his desire to get a bandage on his chief's head.

Chesters aimed his revolver and a whooping Comanche toppled from his pony.

'Good shooting,' Cal praised.

The smoke-charged air was heavy with the acrid greyish-white discharges, the sky was illuminated by the flashes from each gun barrel. Several troopers were congregated by Lieutenant Killeen into small groups behind the natural rampart above the deep draw, where their carbines spat defiant round after round towards the hostiles.

A soldier slipped, almost falling backwards into the draw, his left hand grasping for support as he sought to steady himself. Next to him the body of a colleague lay in a crumpled heap. The trooper's eyes dulled with the sudden realization that it could have been him lying there. He tasted the bile that rose in his throat and, unable to stop himself, threw up, embarrassed at his show of weakness. He looked around quickly to see if any of his fellow defenders had seen, then quickly raised his rifle and added his firepower to the spirited defence already taking place.

Lieutenant Killeen had astutely mixed his men in with those of Captain Chesters and the combined force maintained a steady rate of fire. Volley after volley flew in the direction of the Indians. More Indians were coming from the south to join the attack and, seeing this, Killeen realized his force might be overwhelmed if the hostiles mounted a concentrated attack upon one spot of his defensive line. He voiced his fears to Cal Avery.

The intensity of carbine fire increased as a number of the wounded added their firepower to the ferocity as men fought for their lives. Eventually the sheer intensity of fire from all across the line forced the Indians to retreat and regroup.

From behind the lip of the draw Cal Avery told Killeen of an idea he'd had, a tactic he'd learned during the war. Killeen nodded his agreement and called for every third man to step backwards to create a second line, which Killeen formed into two floating squads, putting Sergeants Coggins and Walters in charge, two men deep in each squad; each able to fire in turn.

Sergeant Walters took his squad to a position behind the right flank. Sergeant Coggins took his to the left. Then without warning a formation of mounted Indians charged the centre of the defensive line.

'Hold your positions,' shouted Lieutenant Killeen, sucking in a lungful of air as he watched the hostiles swarm to the attack. He had formed the floating squads in anticipation of a centre attack and had drilled into the troopers there the necessity to move fast, manoeuvring into a reverse arrowhead to engage the Indian charge in a lethal crossfire.

Many Indian ponies fell to the ground, but a small number managed to break through. Lieutenant Killeen fired his own pistol and slashed his sabre at the first Comanche brave to come close. Then he felt the weapon being dragged from his grasp as he lunged at another warrior. Killeen slipped, almost losing his footing.

The second Indian lay at his feet, dead, Killeen's sabre embedded in his stomach. His unseeing dull eyes stared bleakly up at the lieutenant. The man's mouth was wide open, as though frozen in the act of screaming. Lieutenant Killeen tugged the sword free and pressed forward; weak sunlight glittered on blades of war all around him. He was half-blinded by sweat as he fired his pistol at a galloping Indian pony.

An arrow thumped into the side of the wagon's wooden seat with a sickening thud. Scared witless, Amy Jordan cowered behind the wagon, eyes closed, hands over both ears, not daring to look ahead. More arrows, more shrieks. Where was Cal when she needed him?

Behind her a trooper was loading his carbine. His violent bellow forced her to glance around; an arrow was stuck in the man's neck. A second figure came into view as the trooper began to slip to the ground, his hold on life ebbing away. A bare-chested Comanche loomed out of the gun smoke. A scream choked in her throat as everything seemed to move in slow-motion.

Amy's terror-filled eyes never left the glinting tomahawk blade as it swung through its preparatory backward arc. Her piercing cry filled the air as the muscles in the Comanche's arm bulged, sending the weapon swinging downwards.

The big Colt bucked in Jumbo's hand, sending the Indian hurtling back to crash against the side of the wagon, a large hole in his forehead, from which blood pulsed.

The Indian charge was halted as suddenly as it had begun. The fifty feet of ground in front of the draw was littered with the bodies of the attackers. But the

116

temporary victory had not been gained cheaply: several blue-coated bodies lay motionless.

'Well done, men. Well done. Now hold fast. Keep your eyes peeled!' Killeen yelled.

His words seemed to counter any instinct to retreat, and provided a new incentive.

Cal's hat was gone, and when the Indians had broken through the line he had received a glancing blow from a flashing tomahawk to the side of his temple. It stung unbearably and had forced him to take a staggering half-step backward; however, at that moment the closeness of bodies prevented him from falling. A steadying hand had gripped his arm and helped him regain his balance. The trooper's grinning face came as welcome relief. The soldier handed over Cal's hat with a nod.

Lieutenant Killeen scanned the western terrain minutely. Of the Indians there was no sign. Was it really all over?

His thoughts were interrupted by the ping of a bullet striking the blade of his sabre, knocking the sword from his grasp. A second bullet whined past his cheek; the hostiles had changed their tactics, and were now firing from long range. Far in the distance gun flashes could be seen, at a range too far for a Winchester or a cavalry issue carbine.

Next to Cal a trooper went down, staring wide-eyed, a large bullet hole in his forehead.

'Take cover,' Cal shouted. 'They're using buffalo guns.'

Another trooper was hurled backwards as a bullet took him in the chest.

On a small ridge Lone Elk sat on his pony, directing his horde of braves. He was more than irritated at the spirited defence being put up against overwhelming odds; he had expected to overrun the long knives easily. Now, seeing that he could not dislodge the cavalrymen from the draw he ordered his warriors to draw off, and with a few long-range buffalo guns, turned his attention to the soldiers' horses. Eight horses and oxen suffered death before the Indians ran short of large-bore ammunition and were forced to cease the barrage.

Fighting had continued for most of the day, and the Indians believed they would soon break the spirit of the soldiers; however what Lone Elk didn't know was that the cavalrymen had plenty of ammunition.

In a momentary lull, one of Killeen's troopers, Barney Shaw, his mount, a fine chestnut mare, had once been a fast racer. He told Lieutenant Killeen that he believed he could break through the Indian lines and carry the news of the troopers' plight to Fort Griffin, where he felt sure he could get relief. Killeen commended Shaw for his bravery, but after consideration opposed his suggestion. However, Trooper Shaw would not allow the matter to rest and insisted that Sergeant Coggins should approach the officer again.

Although ammunition was plentiful, the cavalry-men were running low on water, the situation becoming more critical as the blistering Texas sun glared down on them.

Finally Lieutenant Killeen, persuaded by Sergeant Coggins, and unopposed by Cal Avery, relented and allowed Trooper Shaw to make the attempt.

The mare had been sheltered between the wagons in the centre of the draw and had thus avoided the earlier long-range shots of the Indians. Shaw readjusted his saddle and made ready. As he tightened the cinches several men clapped their brave colleague on the back. A fellow trooper noticed that his hands trembled like an aspen leaf, and begged his comrade to reconsider. Ignoring the cavalryman's protestations Trooper Shaw tight-ened his gunbelt, pulled his cavalry hat down tight over his eyes and mounted, careful to push his sabre clear of his legs. Lieutenant Killeen walked over.

'It's not too late to change your mind, Trooper,' he said, regretting his earlier decision to allow the attempt.

'No, sir,' responded Shaw. 'I'm sure I can make it.'

Killeen handed the trooper a note to pass on to the commander at Fort Griffin. He doffed his cap.

'The very best of luck go with you, Trooper Shaw. Ride fast, and don't stop for anything.'

He turned to Sergeant Coggins. 'Pass the word

along the line, on my signal, to open up with all we've got.' Coggins hurried away.

A minute later Killeen fired a shot in the air and every trooper joined in setting up a ferocious barrage.

Trooper Shaw dug his spurs deep into the sides of his mare, and at one bound was out of the draw, galloping south-west at full speed for the open country. His fellow troopers cheered wildly as he sped away.

Old Lone Elk was too wily to be caught napping, and immediately he saw the trooper he sent some of his best mounted warriors off in pursuit. He signalled to his braves at that end of the draw to try to bar the way.

Not having so far to run, the braves in the south quickly spurred forward, closing in on the trooper's zigzagging path.

Cavalrymen fired at the onrushing Indians, attempting to protect Shaw's flight as the best they could, and Dek Lawson, one of Shaw's closest friends, exposed himself a little too much; he was hit in the right elbow by a rifle bullet that shattered the bone and came out at the wrist. The troopers brought down two or three Indians, but their efforts were not enough to save their comrade. The defenders could only watch, hearts full of despair as they saw Trooper Shaw and his mare shot down and killed before they had gone 600 yards.

11

After hours of fierce fighting the Indian attack began to run out of steam, a testimony to the accuracy and ferocity of the defence put up by the cavalrymen.

The dying sun began to dip behind the western hills and the land became cloaked with a blanket of darkness. Lieutenant Killeen walked over to where Cal was crouching. When he saw Captain Chesters he stood stock still, his mouth agape, unbelieving.

Chesters said. 'I trust you do not intend to make a lasting habit of that expression, Lieutenant.'

It was the first attempt at humour they had heard from the captain.

'Yes, sir, Captain.' Killeen saluted.

'Carry on, Lieutenant. I wish you to remain in command.' He looked around. 'Where is—'

Killeen interrupted the captain's question. 'Lieutenant Dakin is dead, sir. Killed in the first charge.' His voice was sad. 'He died bravely, doing his duty.'

Captain Chesters slapped a bloody hand against his thigh.

'Sorry,' Killeen added.

Chesters turned to Cal. 'Avery. Is it true that Indians do not fight at night?'

'Mostly,' answered Cal. 'Better hope it's true of this bunch.'

An eerie silence descended on the battlefield, the overcast purple-black sky devoid of moon and stars. Troopers felt able to relax for the first time for hours. Fires were lit, coffee and hot food prepared. Those troopers on guard peered into the inky blackness, as muffled sounds drifted from the late battlefield in front of the draw. Fingers tightened on triggers as the jumpy sentries fought to stay awake. Men pulled collars up around their necks as a thin protection against the cool Texas night.

Cal Avery and Bob Gates made their way around the camp to reassure the men that the noises they could hear were being made by Indians; squaws mostly, collecting bodies to take for ritual burial.

Having spent a long and nervous night, the sleep deprived troopers awoke to a bright morning. All trace of the Indians had disappeared; the only remaining bodies were those of dead ponies scattered around the scene of the fighting. Of the Comanches and Kiowas there was no trace.

Cal and Killeen stood on the scarred raised lip on the edge of the draw, hands on hips, watching their own burial detail consign many brave men to a makeshift grave. Captain Chesters sat against a nearby rock. None of the three spoke for some time; each of them was drained and exhausted, as showed clearly on their ashen faces.

Eventually Killeen spoke up. 'Can you explain it?'

Cal frowned. 'I've heard of it, but never experienced it.'

'Could it be because we killed so many of them?'

'I don't think so,' Cal opined. 'Don't plan on catching up with them to ask,' he joked grimly.

Lieutenant Killeen turned to look at Captain Chesters. The captain's head had slumped on to his chest.

'Asleep?' queried Cal.

Killeen nodded. 'Better get him somewhere warm, where he can rest.' He called two troopers to help carry the captain to Jumbo's wagon.

When the troopers lifted the captain they saw how his cavalry blouse was drenched in blood; the stain was still wet as blood pulsed from under the captain's left arm; his face was ashen.

'Get Schmidt. Quick.' Killeen ordered. He feared for Chesters, the officer looked to be knocking loudly at death's door. Killeen felt powerless to intervene in the captain's struggle for life. He took off his tunic and spread it across Chesters's motionless body.

Schmidt arrived, looking drawn and exhausted. The small orderly knelt beside Captain Chesters's supine body, setting down a heavy canvas bag full of bandages and potions. He handed the tunic to Lieutenant Killeen and carefully unbuttoned the captain's blouse, opening the garment, spreading it wide, meticulously moving aside the bloodstained shirt beneath.

The captain's skin was pale as death except on his left side, which was covered in scarlet wetness. With a most gentle touch Schmidt dabbed at the source of the bleeding, mopping the fresh blood away to reveal two bullet holes. He looked up, 'I will need help.'

'Can we move him?'

'No!' Schmidt almost shouted, then went to work. He plugged the bullet holes and applied pads of gauze like material soaked in some liquid he had taken from his medical bag. He held up a broad roll of bandage. 'I need to wrap this bandage round his wounds.'

The two soldiers, instructed by the orderly, raised the captain's limp body, Lieutenant Killeen holding the shirt and blouse out of the way. Schmidt nodded and began to wrap the bandage as tightly as he could, sweat pouring from his narrow brow, threatening to run into his eyes. Cal picked up a cloth and mopped the sweat from the orderly's forehead.

'Thank you,' said Schmidt.

When he was finished the orderly stood up, satisfied with his work. He stretched his legs, rubbing some life back into the cramped muscles.

Schmidt turned to Lieutenant Killeen; his voice

held no emotion, 'I have done all I can. He is in God's hands now.'

'Will he live?' Killeen asked softly.

'Only God knows the answer to that question, sir.' Schmidt put on his forage cap, thought for a moment then added, 'The bullets are still inside the captain's body. There were no exit wounds. I have done all I can. He needs a surgeon.'

'The nearest surgeon is at Fort Griffin,' said Killeen. 'Is he strong enough to make that journey?'

The orderly reflected. 'We shall need to fashion a stretcher. A large flat piece of wood.'

A trooper ran off towards the wagons. He returned with a tailgate. 'This do?'

Schmidt nodded. 'Lay it next to the captain. We must slide him on to it and lash him on tight.'

Cal and Killeen helped the troopers follow the orderly's instructions.

'Gently now!' Schmidt cried out.

The captain seemed to be barely breathing. His body was strapped securely to the makeshift stretcher, and carried slowly to Jumbo's wagon. Various boxes and sacks had been moved to the other wagon to make room.

After Captain Chesters's body had been placed inside, Lieutenant Killeen dusted down his stained uniform and set his kepi on his head.

'Sergeant Coggins,' he called out. 'Have all non-commissioned officers brought to me. Then assemble the men for inspection in fifteen minutes.'

He explained the situation to the NCOs and told them what he expected of them. Of the fifty-four officers and men, thirty-nine had survived; five of those were in no condition to ride; they would have to travel in the wagons.

The two Quaker wagons were where they had been abandoned, four of the eight oxen were found none the worse for wear, and were hitched to a wagon. Spare horses were hitched to the second Quaker wagon. Enough of the mules were still alive to make up one team; spare horses were used for the other.

So, one hour after noon, Lieutenant Killeen leading, the wagon train set off on its journey to Fort Griffin.

Cal looked around. 'Where's Elkins?'

'Haven't seen him since the first Indian charge,' said Killeen.'

It was the same story with everyone Cal asked. No one had seen the Elkins. All three of them had disappeared.

In the back of Jumbo's wagon Captain Chesters's wounds continued to bleed. Orderly Schmidt changed the dressings as regularly as he could. One of the Quaker wives washed the dirty bandages once the column had replenished its water supplies.

The cavalrymen were in relatively good spirits as they began the journey to Fort Griffin. Lieutenant Dakin had been buried with the other dead at the head of the ravine; a large cairn had been built to

126

mark their grave. That night the company camped at the mouth of Devil's Creek.

The following morning, Lieutenant Killeen instructed Corporal Gates to detail two troopers and, with a pack-mule, to make their way to the head of Devil's Creek, where Cal had felt sure they would find some stray cattle, to kill one and bring the beef back.

Lieutenant Killeen's caravan reached Fort Griffin shortly after nightfall. The fortress stood on a small knoll overlooking the Clear Fork tributary of the Brazos River. The stockade walls and most of the buildings were of timber construction, except on the north side of the parade ground where three or four adobe-brick huts stood. Dotted around were a blacksmith's forge next to corrals for livestock; storerooms, workshops, and barracks.

Keen-eyed lookouts waved to the newcomers from two tall watchtowers on either side of the main gate: midnight-blue figures silhouetted by flaming torches and oil lamps. The huge gates swung open with a massive groan.

Captain Chesters was taken to the fort's infirmary. Lieutenant Killeen went off to deliver his report to the camp commandant.

Amy Jordan was left at the army post, where the commandant's wife promised to look after her. The news that her brother had fully recovered from his long illness was music to her ears. However a reunion would have to wait until he returned from patrol.

Cal and Jumbo made sure she was settled comfortably, then decided to go into town where a reviving drink beckoned; in any case Cal would need to go to the Ranger Station to make his own report.

Before he left Amy kissed him on the cheek and thanked him for all he had done for her. He promised to return for dinner with her, the commandant and his wife.

The frontier settlement known locally as The Flat was a sorry excuse for a town. In no way could the place be described as prosperous-looking. The Flat masqueraded as a cowtown, a centre of buffalo hunting, populated by whores, skinners and gamblers.

Cal and Jumbo rode leisurely down what passed for Main Street to the small Texas Ranger station sited at the opposite end of the settlement to the fort. Sandwiching The Flat between two centres of law and order would appear to have been a good idea; however things do not always work like that in practice, and The Flat was a lawless place.

12

Cal Avery turned away in disgust. Major Webster had remained unshaken in his opinion when the ranger had delivered his report.

'Well? What did he say?' Jumbo Jepson had waited patiently for his friend outside Ranger divisional headquarters.

Cal frowned. 'Wouldn't change his mind,' he said bitterly. 'Said I had no choice but to argue my innocence in court.'

Jumbo cursed loudly. 'Let's go get that drink.'

The two men left their horses at the Ranger station and walked into town. They pushed open the batwing doors of the first saloon they came to. Few drinkers in the sparsely attended bar-room bothered to waste a glance in the direction of the newcomers.

Jumbo slapped a calloused hand on the beer-stained bar.

'Whiskey,' he demanded. The bartender poured

out two shot glasses. 'Leave the bottle,' Jumbo told him.

Cal looked around the bar, sizing up their fellow drinkers. A couple of rough-looking cowboys leaned on the bar at one end. They had dirty calloused hands and fingernails, neither had shaved in several days. A cocktail of mud and cow dung stuck to their scuffed boots, the rowels on their spurs were worn down. All telltale signs of working cowboys. They ambled over to a table; one of the two limped – they didn't pose any kind of threat.

The level in the whiskey bottle quickly fell from full to half-empty in double-quick time.

Cal swirled the amber liquid around the glass and, lowering his voice, said, 'They got me, Jumbo.' He glowered. 'There's no way I can prove it wasn't me.'

Jumbo grabbed his friend's arm. 'Now, Cal, that ain't like you.' He ran a finger over his lower lip, trying to think of something positive to say, concentration furrowed his craggy brow. 'Don't you go givin' up just yet.'

Behind them, the batwing doors banged open and shut. A nervy silence descended on the dim interior of the saloon. One or two drinkers got up and left. Jumbo looked round to see who had come in. He stiffened and nudged Cal's arm.

The voice was deep. 'I'll take your pistol, Cal.'

Cal recognized the southern drawl of town marshal, Joe Hines. The ranger turned slowly;

hooking a boot heel over the tarnished brass footrail, Cal leaned back against the bar, both elbows on the wooden surface.

Marshal Hines held out a piece of white paper towards Cal. His craggy face was set in a solemn expression.

'Got a warrant for your arrest.'

Cal eyed the warrant with obvious disdain.

The marshal's buzzard-like eyes flickered round the room, taking in the entire scene as he anticipated trouble, ready if it came. The lawman's feet were planted firmly on the sawdust-covered floorboards, his right hand hovered over the butt of his Colt. Only the slightest twitching of his drooping moustache betrayed any hint of nervousness.

'I don't want to do this. Don't even agree with it,' Marshal Hines said apologetically. 'But it's my job.'

Still Cal said nothing.

'Don't want any trouble, Cal.' The marshal's face grew even dimmer. 'It's your call. I ask you like a friend to give me your pistol.' Marshal Hines moved his right hand away from his Colt and extended it towards the ranger, palm upwards.

The atmosphere in the dingy saloon was electric; had a pin been dropped it would have been heard. It was obvious to all that Cal Avery was considering his options.

Cal Avery had known Joe Hines for longer than five years. He had shared many a drink with him; they had chased and fought hostiles and renegades together. Now he faced a man he was proud to call a friend in a bizarre face-off. Cal hated the thought of giving in without a fight; it had never been his way to tiptoe around situations, but this was different; drawing against a long-standing friend was abhorrent to him.

Marshal Hines was showing all the patience of his forty-eight years.

Cal's furrowed brow showed no other real emotion; so far he had given no indication of what he might do.

The two men stood facing each other for many minutes, neither moving a muscle. The atmosphere could have been cut with a knife. Jumbo was tongue-tied, wanting to help his friend, but not knowing how.

Suddenly Cal Avery unhooked his boot heel, breaking the eerie silence as his foot hit the floor. Joe Hines stiffened.

'All right, Joe,' Cal said. 'I'll give you my gun. But not until we get inside your jailhouse. OK?'

For a moment the marshal's flint-grey eyes widened.

'OK,' he said after considering the offer. 'Let's go.'

Cal and Jumbo downed what was left of the whiskey the teamster had been pouring when the marshal's entrance interrupted him, then followed the lawman out of the saloon.

'Trial's set for next Monday,' Marshal Hines told

them as they walked along the boardwalk.

There were more folks than usual out on the street as people heard the news of the face-off between the marshal and the ranger.

'Lawyer O'Halloran is insisting on defending you. Says he owes you,' Hines added.

'He's a good man,' said Cal.

'He's waiting at the jail,' Joe Hines told him. 'Judge Hollins gets in Sunday afternoon.'

'Judge Hollins?' exclaimed Cal.

'That a problem?'

'Ain't good,' Cal answered. 'Me and him aren't exactly bosom pals.'

Cal's three days and nights in jail proved to be uneventful. A lot of time was spent with his lawyer, going over the events of the day in question, trying to put together an adequate defence, attempting to construct an hour-by-hour account of Cal's movements. Witnesses were contacted, affidavits taken and recorded.

Among Cal's numerous visitors was Amy Jordan; she came on three separate occasions, always in the company of Lieutenant Killeen. Jumbo called in a couple of times. So did Sergeant Coggins and Major Webster.

On her second visit Amy took Cal's big hand in hers, her pretty face was bathed in a smile of contentment. She kissed him on the lips when she left.

*

The trial began at nine a.m. on Monday in the saloon bar of the Cattleman's Hotel.

Judge Hollins, resplendent in a black frock-coat and high-winged collar, entered the noisy court-room from a side room; under one arm he carried a large black Bible. The neatly knotted narrow black string tie contrasted sharply with the white shirt he wore. His thinning white hair crowned a pleasant face of ruddy complexion, his thick lips appeared to set his mouth in a permanent smile. His dignified appearance was aided by a well-trimmed salt-and-pepper moustache and beard. Judge Hollins took great pride in his perfectly groomed appearance.

'All rise,' called out the bailiff as Judge Hollins climbed the three steps to his seat on the specially constructed dais.

The judge nodded to the bailiff and the legal representatives and took his seat. He picked up a huge wooden gavel and brought it down heavily on a solid block of wood.

The bailiff coughed once to clear his throat and announced. 'This court is now in session. The Honourable Judge Hollins presiding.'

'Please be seated,' Hollins said in a deep booming bass voice, at odds with his thin and frail-looking frame. 'Let us pray,' he continued.

Following the reciting of the Lord's Prayer, the twelve-man jury was sworn in, and the charge read out, defendant and plaintiff identified, and opening statements made.

Witness after witness swore, three in all, on oath that they had seen Cal Avery gun down Billy Elkins in cold blood, and later had seen the same man cowardly shoot Billy's cousin, Deke Juggins, in the back. Cal Avery was seen walking after Juggins, rifle in hand; he was operating the lever to load the gun. The story never varied in the slightest detail.

'All been well coached,' whispered O'Halloran. Cal knew it wasn't going well. He turned to look around the courtroom; none of the Elkins clan was there to see the profit of their bribery come to fruition. Cal's eyes lit on Lieutenant Killeen, Amy Jordan alongside him; she flashed him a wonderful smile, which made his heart leap.

When the final prosecution witness had stepped down two men at the back of the courtroom stood up.

'Excuse me Your Honour. Mind if I speak?' asked one of the men.

'Come forward.' Judge Hollins beckoned. 'Swear him in, bailiff. Give your name, and tell the court what you know.'

The new witness was obviously nervous, but his voice was clear.

'The fellers I just heard claiming to have witnessed Avery shooting that kid aren't telling the truth, Your Honour.'

'Go on,' said Judge Hollins.

The man nodded. 'Me and Jim there,' he pointed to the other man standing at the back of the court, 'we saw Waco, Smith, and Texas in the Phoenix saloon, Jake Elkins's place, on that evening. They were drinking a lot and playing poker from a little after noon till late that night. So there's no way any of 'em could have seen Avery shoot that kid.'

Judge Hollins stroked his beard. 'What makes you so sure what you are saying is correct?'

'Because me and Jim were playing with them. Ask the bartender. I can name at least five other people that saw them with us.'

A huge gasp surged around the court.

The second man was sworn in; his evidence was the same as the first man's.

'Why did you not come forward earlier?' Judge Hollins enquired of the second man.

'We're both cow-punchers, Judge. Been out on the range since that night. Just got back to town, heard about the trial and decided we ought to come to the court and speak up.'

The prosecutor took a crack at the two cowboys without success.

'Are either of you acquainted with the defendant?' Judge Hollins asked the cowhands.

'Only know of him by reputation, Your Honour.'

'You may step down.'

Cal looked hopefully at his lawyer. O'Halloran shrugged and called his character witnesses.

A relieved Cal Avery didn't want to contemplate what might have been the outcome if those two public-spirited cowboys had not turned up.

One or two titters rang out when Jumbo Jepson took the stand, silenced by a rap from the judge's gavel.

'No, sir. There's no way on this earth Cal Avery would backshoot anybody.' Jumbo blew his nose loudly. 'Why, he's the most upstandin', law-abidin' man I ever knew.'

Lieutenant Killeen added his praise to that of Jumbo's, testifying to Cal's honesty and trustworthiness.

Amy Jordan, looking downright pretty, told the court how Cal Avery had rescued her from the Comanches.

Even Captain Chesters from his sick bed in the hospital at Fort Griffin sent his own sworn affidavit supporting the notion of Cal's honesty and bravery.

Then it was Cal's turn to take the stand.

'Judge,' he said, 'I will admit to shooting Billy Elkins, but I swear I did not shoot Deke Juggins. I shot Billy fair and square. The two of them ambushed me, took a couple of shots at me, one creased my forearm.' He rolled up his sleeve to show the recent scar. 'I flushed them out and tried to arrest them. Billy refused to be arrested, and went for his six-gun.'

Judge Hollins interrupted. 'Just to clarify. You say Billy Elkins drew first?'

'Yes, Your Honour. His first bullet passed through the sleeve of my coat. He wouldn't reason with me, just yanked out his gun and fired off a shot. When he took aim for a second shot, I drew my own pistol and shot him. Young Deke ran away. I did not pursue him. Exactly who bushwhacked him I could not say.' Cal took a breath. 'I stayed with Billy, having sent for a doctor.'

Adrian Morley, the county prosecutor, wasn't about to give up without a fight. 'Is it not true that a feud exists between you and the Elkins family, and that you conduct a personal vendetta against Jake Elkins?'

Cal looked at the judge.

'Objection!' O'Halloran called out.

'Overruled. Answer the question,' Judge Hollins ordered.

Cal searched for the right words. 'I will admit there is bad blood between the Elkins and me, but there is no vendetta.'

Morley tried hard, but could not shake Cal's testimony any more than he could that of any of the defence witnesses, and Cal was allowed to step down.

Lawyer O'Halloran called Doctor Mackenzie.

'Your Honour, my opinion is that the kid, sorry, Deke Juggins, was shot by someone using a large-bore rifle, fifty calibre at least. A big gun that left a big hole, possibly the kind a buffalo hunter would use. I dug this slug out of the body.'

He ferreted around in his waistcoat pocket and fetched out a spent bullet which he dropped into an empty glass on the judge's desk with a loud tinkle.

'Judge, may I offer something which you may or may not think relevant to the shooting of Deke Juggins.'

'Proceed.'

'I was the doctor who attended Billy Elkins, and I can state with all honesty that Cal Avery stayed with me until the undertaker collected the body. We both, and the large crowd that had arrived, heard a single loud gunshot which I believe was the shot that killed Deke, whom I also attended. I had been summoned when I was on my way back to my surgery, so I went from the scene of one fatal shooting to the next, as it were. Cal Avery was out of my sight for only a matter of a few minutes, and only after we had heard that loud gunshot.

'Between then and being summoned to attend Deke I can categorically state that I heard no further discharges from any other weapon. Therefore in my eyes there is no way Cal Avery could have possibly bushwhacked Deke Juggins. No way,' Doctor Mackenzie repeated.

The doctor stepped down, and prosecution and defence lawyers made their closing remarks. O'Halloran concentrated on the large bore weapon and the timings mentioned by the doctor, asserting that it was well known that his client favoured a Winchester, and had never owned or been seen carrying a large-bore buffalo gun.

The judge summed up and instructed the jury on

the relevant points of law. Then he sent them out to deliberate. It took less than twenty minutes for the jury to reach a decision. They returned a verdict of not guilty.

Judge Hollins thanked everyone for attending and closed the proceedings. He was taking a late lunch break, he said before tackling the next case: a serious allegation against a drifter, namely the theft of two hogs. Of selling one, and eating the other.

Cal shook the judge's hand warmly.

'I'm not used to seeing you in the dock, Avery,' said the judge. 'Don't care to see you there again.'

Cal smiled. 'Be seeing you, Judge.'

Later that evening, when the final rays of copper-coloured sunlight slanted through windows coated on the outside with dust and smoke-stains on the inside, and after the courtroom had been converted back to a saloon bar, Cal Avery approached the county prosecutor at the bar.

'Morley,' he challenged loudly, already knowing the answer to his next question, 'I want to know who it was who set me up.' Lamps were being lit as Cal's huge shadow covered the lawyer.

Behind the bar, bottles and glasses tinkled as the bartender wiped down the shelves. A uneasy hush descended; men sensed trouble. Adrian Morley shook Cal's hand off his arm.

'You know I cannot divulge confidential information, Cal.' His false smile fooled no one. 'Have a drink? Let's be fiends?'

Cal eyed the prosecutor, fury raging in his eyes. 'No thanks, Morley. You and me will never be friends as long as you're in cahoots with the Elkins.'

Morley bridled at Cal's veiled accusation. 'That's a barefaced lie and you know it.'

'Then, sir, I am at your disposal. Weapons of your choice.' Cal knew he was letting himself down, but despite a voice inside him imploring him to be silent, the challenge just kind of slipped out, accidentally on purpose.

Morley's face blanched; there was no way he would ever agree to taking on Cal Avery. He downed the glass of whiskey in front of him, needing to buy time to think, and to take the edge off his fear.

'We are on the same side of the law. We work together,' he bleated.

'Jake Elkins's comeuppance is on its way. If you stay on his side, yours is on its way too.'

'I am not and never have been in cahoots with Jake Elkins. You are misinformed.'

'Am I?' Cal challenged. 'You've been on the take for years. Elkins has paid you plenty. And now you've opened up the can of worms I aim to prove it, if it's the last thing I do.'

Morley laughed nervously, aware of the crowd of influential people listening in.

'Avery, if you think you can prove anything, let's you and me go see Judge Hollins.'

'Not today. But one day soon, Morley, you'll make a slip and I'll be waiting.'

Cal turned on his heel and stalked out of the saloon.

13

'Cal. Have you heard?' It was Jumbo Jepson running to catch up with his friend as he left the saloon.

'Heard what?'

'Baxter Elkins and his gang rode in about an hour ago. Heard it from a feller down at the livery stable.'

'Where are they?'

'I'm not sure. He told me he thought he'd seen 'em go into the Phoenix.'

'Jake Elkins's place. Figures. How many?'

'He said he couldn't be certain. Three for sure. Might have been four. He didn't hang around to find out, but he recognized the old man, together with the two Blackhouse brothers.'

'Waco and Tex, huh?' Cal rubbed his chin. 'So with Jake and Kyle that's the entire clan.'

'No. Kyle took a Comanche bullet in his spine when they deserted us at the ravine. According to the doc, he won't walk again. And Jake's nephews are still in the state pen. So can't be more'n five, maybe six.'

Cal hesitated, trying to formulate a plan. 'I'm going to see Major Webster at the Ranger station.'

'I just came from there, lookin' for you,' said Jumbo. 'Major took his men out earlier. Some Comanches raided a coupla ranches, took a couple of females hostage. There's only old Mose and the wrangler left.'

Cal held back his curse. 'Do you know if Joe Hines is in his office?'

'No.'

'Let's go see.'

'Cal, I can't drop everything just like that.' Marshal Hines glanced over his shoulder, he was loading a double-barrelled shotgun. 'I got enough trouble of my own without looking for more. There's a bunch of rowdy buffalo hunters and skinners down at the Golden Star I got to go sort out. My two deputies are already on their way down there. That has to take precedence. Sorry. Can't be helped.' He saw Cal's hangdog expression. 'Be happy to help when I've got this bunch sorted.'

'Can I borrow a Winchester, Marshal? Mine's down at the hotel.'

'What? You ain't planning to go up against the entire gang, are you?'

'I gotta go see what they're up to. I may never have a better chance to collar them.'

Marshal Hines stopped him, barring the way to the door with the shotgun.

'Leave the Winchester,' he ordered, frowning. 'Cal. This is my town. Technically you ain't got no jurisdiction here, so I can't let you go starting a shooting contest. I won't allow it. Also, there's no papers on any of the Elkins gang in this town. So I'm telling you straight. Either wait here for me, or go on back to the hotel and I'll see what we can sort out later.' He smiled an avuncular smile. 'Agreed?'

Cal looked deep into the old lawman's eyes, knowing he was right, but hating it.

'Agreed,' he said.

The marshal turned and left the office. 'See you later then. And Cal' – the ranger turned – 'try and keep out of trouble, huh?'

Cal shrugged innocently and opened the door. Once out in the street, he said to Jumbo. 'Let's get back to the hotel, then get a drink.'

At the hotel he left Jumbo waiting in the lobby and took the stairs three at a time. The Winchester was in the corner leaning against the wall where he had left it. Cal picked the rifle up, the wooden stock felt warm to his touch. He operated the lever to check that the weapon was fully loaded and repeated the action with his Colt and the thirty-eight that he took from his saddle-bags.

The urgent rap on the door was loud. Cal thumbed back the hammer on the thirty-eight and moved to the door, careful to keep clear of the line of fire should whoever was knocking decide to fire off a couple of rounds through the door.

'Who is it?' he called out.

'It's me. Jumbo.'

'You alone?'

'Sure.'

Cal turned the key and opened the door a fraction. 'What do you want?'

'What?' Jumbo flashed Cal an irritated look. 'What do you mean, what do I want? I'm going with you, you big ape.'

The ranger shook his head. 'Not this time, Jumbo, this ain't your fight.' Jumbo's face creased with annoyance. 'Besides which, you aren't any match with a gun for Elkins and his gunslingers. No offence,' Cal added.

'But you can't go alone, there's too many of 'em,' Jumbo protested.

'No more than I've faced before.'

'How can you say that? You don't even know for sure how many men Elkins has got with him.'

Before Cal could respond there was another knock at the door. This time it was Lieutenant Killeen; with him were Sergeant Coggins and Corporal Gates. All three were out of uniform, toting repeating rifles, gunbelts tied down.

'What do you three want?'

Killeen answered, 'We're coming with you.'

Cal began to protest, but the lieutenant held up a hand to silence him.

146

'Nothing you can say will change our minds; we're coming and that's that. What's the plan?'

'Plan? There is no plan,' Cal retorted. For a moment all was silent, then Cal relented, his heart filled with emotion, touched by these men's offer to help.

The five men combed every inch of the town systematically, but none of the Elkins gang were seen. Reluctantly the three cavalrymen returned to the fort, leaving a lasting promise of help whenever Cal wanted it. Jumbo suggested a quick drink before supper. Cal admitted he was ready for one.

The air inside the saloon was smoky and dark. Before Cal had moved one step, a heady aroma of unwashed bodies mixed with those of rot-gut whiskey and stale beer smacked his nostrils. An abundance of dim lanterns spiralled plumes of smoke into the rafters of the low ceiling, depositing sooty smudges on to those who had gone before them. A few inquisitive eyes moved in their direction, then turned away, satisfied that the newcomers weren't threatening.

Jumbo sidled through the half-drunken crowd of cowboys to the trestle supported by two large barrels, which served for a bar. Catching the eye of the barman he banged down a couple of coins on the bar, ordering whiskey.

A once-pretty soiled dove with a cast in her right eye wandered over as the bartender deposited a bottle and two shot glasses on to the bar. Running one finger over the top of her large half-exposed breasts, she whispered hoarsely,

'Will you gentlemen be wanting anything else?' Jumbo noticed that her wrists were covered in bruises.

'Not right now,' he replied politely. Cal ignored her.

The two friends took a seat in the corner and swallowed a mouthful of whiskey.

'God, that's awful,' remarked Jumbo, pulling a face. He poured out two more. Another soiled dove ambled over, this one younger and prettier than the other. She sat down on Jumbo's knee.

'How are you, big fella?'

Cal glanced around the darkened bar room. His gaze rested on one of the many occupants of a table set in the opposite corner. His hand tightened around the glass as his memory exploded with the recognition of a hated face from the past.

The same crescent-shaped scar over his left eye. The unkempt beard, half-hiding the sneering expression. It couldn't be anyone else. Sure, he was older and much heavier in build, but despite the roughness of his appearance Cal was certain that he was looking at an old adversary. No doubt about it. It was Kid McCoy!

Seeing no profit in the two men the saloon girl melted away.

Cal nudged Jumbo, nodding his head slightly in

McCoy's direction.

'Jumbo,' he whispered, 'see the fellow with the scar on his face? The one sitting in the corner wearing the bowler hat.'

'Yeah. What about him?' Jumbo queried, taking a drink.

'I'm sure I know him, and by all that's right he should not be here.'

'Why not?'

The man in the bowler hat got to his feet and made to leave the saloon.

Cal watched the man and answered Jumbo's question. 'Because he used to ride with the Elkins gang. That's why not.'

'Does he know you?' asked Jumbo.

'He sure does. I gave him that scar.'

'Watch out! He's coming over,' Cal whispered, raising a hand in front of his face in an attempt to avoid recognition.

Kid McCoy paused before reaching their table to allow the squint-eyed soiled dove to get out of his way. He groped her breasts as she passed and slapped her ample rump, sneering out a wicked laugh as the woman aimed a swipe at his face. McCoy easily blocked the blow with his arm, then turned on his heel, heading towards the exit. A lantern illuminated his cruel face as he tugged his battered bowler hat low on his forehead.

He passed close enough for Cal to confirm it was the McCoy he knew. Not that he needed much confirmation: every fibre of his body was filled with hatred. The batwing doors creaked open and shut, and McCoy was gone into the darkness of the night.

'Come on, Jumbo, I want to see what he's up to.'

Jumbo followed his friend to the door. Cal pushed one half of the batwings open gingerly and stepped out into the narrow street. There was enough lamplight to see McCoy turn off the street a few buildings away. The monotonous clump-clump of his boot heels on the wooded boardwalk echoed from wall to wall.

The two friends followed cautiously through the twists and turns of a myriad of narrow alleys, ever deeper into the maze of ill-lit streets, mostly dark save for the reflected moonlight, which brought a kind of silver glow to the buildings. Occasionally McCoy disappeared into shadows, emerging from the darkness soon after.

Suddenly they had a problem. McCoy disappeared into the shadow of a building, but failed to reappear. Cal feared they had lost their quarry. They waited in the shadows a while, but McCoy was nowhere to be seen.

'Damn, we lost him.' Disappointedly Cal decided to return to the hotel. That was, if he could find it, for the moon had now disappeared behind grey clouds. Cal thought he knew the town layout reasonably well, but with so many new buildings going up amidst the dark labyrinth of houses and warehouses, he was suddenly not so sure.

'This way.' he announced, tugging Jumbo's sleeve. 'I can't see any stars, but I hope I can navigate our way back to the hotel.'

Jumbo followed closely as Cal groped along a narrow alley that stank almost overpoweringly of tanned leather and animal skins. The rank odours drifting on the light breeze reminded Cal of cities back East.

The light improved briefly as the moon edged from behind a cloud sufficiently for them to see they had entered what appeared to be a small square with buildings on all four sides; sharply angled roofs sloped down towards the centre. The shuffling sound of uneasy cattle drifted on the night air, coupled with the well-recognized bovine smell.

A dim light shone out like a beacon in the distance. A few strides and they had reached a corral. Instantly Cal recognized where he was: the way back to Main Street was dead ahead.

'It's this way,' he told Jumbo and turned to head confidently back to Main Street.

A lantern opened suddenly, flooding their faces with light, stopping both friends in their tracks. The vivid light shone in their eyes, partially blinding them. A second lantern opened.

A voice broke the stillness. 'Well now. Lookee here! If it ain't that stinking ranger.'

Cal's hand moved towards his six-gun.

'Don' try it, Avery. There's three rifles trained on your no-good back.' Bax Elkins stepped forward a pace into the glow of the second lantern, its beam cutting across his sneering face. Elkins chuckled. Cal and Jumbo said nothing.

'You should've seen the look on your face in the saloon when you recognized me,' McCoy called out from the shadows. 'Nearly wet myself.'

Jumbo didn't know Kid McCoy, but he knew him by reputation: a vicious killer. He touched Cal's arm to signal his friend to make no move; these men were far too cocky.

'Where's that poxy little brother of yours?' McCoy taunted. 'Skulking about with the rest of your vermin, I expect.' McCoy fingered the long deep scar on his cheek, which Cal had put there years earlier during the fight at Fort Arizona in defence of a woman's honour.

Cal stiffened at the insult, feeling the pressure of Jumbo's grip on his arm.

'Hold, Cal, there's more to this situation than we see,' Jumbo whispered.

'Perceptive cuss, ain't you,' said Elkins, his voice even and confident. 'Now *amigos*, it's time to show yourselves.'

Suddenly four other lanterns were uncovered. Each sputtered and dimmed briefly before brightening again to cast grotesque silhouettes, illuminating the faces of the assailants, and Bax Elkins in particular; each shadow making the faces appear even more sinister.

The two friends looked at each other, then all

around them. They were surrounded by at least six of the Elkins gang.

Bax Elkins laughed heartily.

Jake Elkins came to stand at his cousin's shoulder. 'How's that pretty little piece of fluff?'

Jumbo's grip on Cal's arm tightened even more as Jake Elkins continued: 'What *was* her name? Amy something, wasn't it?' Jake was enjoying himself. 'Well, never mind, she weren't nobody special.' He sneered. 'Just like that no-count brother of yours.'

The red mist descended instantly. Cal wrenched his arm away from Jumbo's grip and sprang at Elkins.

The speed and ferocity of the attack took everyone by surprise, including Jumbo who was unable to hold on to his friend's arm. Cal crashed into Jake Elkins and the two men staggered backwards.

Jumbo tried but failed to draw his six-gun as a couple of the Elkins gang jumped on him, the pistol falling some way away.

Before the lights went out in Cal's head he managed to head-butt Elkins. He dived on him, hands searching for and finding his enemy's throat; he squeezed the bristly flesh hard. That was when Cal became aware of the pain, caused by two or three blows raining down on the back of his head. He felt he was being pushed into a long dark tunnel that seemed to have no end.

In the confused mêlée Jumbo fared much better than his friend. He kicked away one man and shoved the second of the men attacking him backwards to give himself some room. Lanterns were dropped hurriedly, casting even more shadows around the small area of open ground. In the corral frightened horses milled around noisily.

Now Jumbo drew his Bowie knife and moved to the attack. Both of the men facing him were big, and undoubtedly strong, but lumberingly slow, and no match for Jumbo's skill with a blade. After stabbing one man in the leg he slashed the other across the face, not knowing how much damage he had done until he heard a sharp cry of pain and felt something wet run down his arm.

Jumbo saw Cal go down and rushed at his friend's attackers. There were at least four of them. One turned as Jumbo slashed at him; his blade jarred against steel as the man managed to parry the cut with his own knife, but failed to see Jumbo's dagger as it buried itself deep into the folds of his stomach. The man grasped at the weapon and Jumbo felt it being wrenched from his grip; a sharp tug and the blade came free.

More lanterns clattered to the ground with a crash as others turned to meet Jumbo's attack. One man raised a pistol, but was off balance as he pulled the trigger and the bullet sailed harmlessly into a wall, flattening itself on impact.

Now Jumbo was amongst them, moving with surprising speed for such a big man, bodies intertwined, the broad-bladed Bowie knife seemingly darting everywhere. A man swung a rifle, but this was no weapon for a fight at close quarters. Jumbo ducked, catching the weapon as it passed his shoulder, expertly flicking the rifle away from the man's grasp as though it were no more than a light cane. He punched the man in the face, slashing the big knife across the man's throat as he fell back. Some sort of cudgel glanced off his left shoulder as he dragged a tomahawk from the back of his belt and backswung the fiendish weapon with all his strength. His arm stung as the weapon sliced open the man's flesh to grate on bone.

Torches flared, and the sound of more men running towards the fight was accompanied by wild shouts. Jake Elkins realized things weren't going his way and called to his men to get away.

The crowd of running men was headed by Marshal Joe Hines and his two deputies. Shots echoed into the night, and two would-be escapers hit the dirt.

'Over here!' shouted Jumbo, lancing another escaping man with his knife, pulling his adversary to the ground into a shadowy part of the yard, his booted foot across the man's neck. He breathed a sigh of relief.

'Good to see you, Marshal,' he called out.

Some of the newcomers chased after the ambushers, and for a moment all was silent and still. Jumbo and the marshal listened intently to the sounds of the pursuit, but soon silence was punctuated only by a few groans from wounded men.

'Let's get these miscreants down to the jail.'

Both injured men were moaning. One protested he was dying. The other moaned, 'Help me, I can't see. I've been cut across my eye.'

Cal Avery was helped unsteadily to his feet and the attackers were marched to the jail.

When all were safely under lock and key and the wounded had been attended by Doctor Mackenzie, the two dead men were taken away by the undertaker. The doc went with them.

An hour later Marshal Hines's two deputies returned carrying a mortally wounded man.

'It's Jake Elkins, Marshal. He stopped to take a shot at us. We couldn't see who it was, Fred had no choice but to shoot him.'

'Take him to the doc's.'

'Don't think he'll make it that far.'

'Go get the doc, then.'

Jake Elkins was dead by the time the doctor arrived.

Cal and Jumbo gratefully accepted a reviving brandy from the marshal.

'Lucky we came along when we did.'

Cal nodded, 'Old Man Elkins suckered me into a trap like a virgin bride.'

Marshal Hines pushed the brandy bottle in Jumbo's direction. The teamster poured himself another.

'Thanks, Marshal. You're a gent.'

Marshal Hines rolled a smoke, 'I'm glad Jake Elkins was with 'em. Won't be many mourning that snake.' He blew a smoke ring. 'Shame we didn't get Bax.'

'Once the lights went out I didn't see what happened,' Cal said with a shrug, 'but I'll get the old buzzard. You can count on that.'

The marshal reflected, sucking in another mouthful of smoke. 'Strange, though. Why they didn't bushwhack you. Must have wanted to give you a good beating first. Make you feel some pain.' He blew out the smoke. 'Either way, you did well to fight 'em off.'

Cal grinned. 'They underestimated my partner there.' He nodded his head towards Jumbo. 'But for him they'd have got me.'

Jumbo looked embarrassed. 'You did your bit,' he said. There was a knock at the door.

'Come in,' the marshal yelled, one hand on his six-gun.

The door opened. It was Amy, Alvin Killeen behind her.

'Nagged me till I agreed to bring her here,' the lieutenant explained.

Amy blushed. 'I was worried,' she confessed. She removed her gloves, and laid a hand on Cal's. She gazed into his eyes; the look on her face said everything.

Cal knew now where his future lay. His heart was full.

The door opened again. Doctor MacKenzie's head popped around.

'Thought you'd like to know, Marshal. When I got back to my surgery there were two men waiting for me. Both had serious wounds, bleeding badly. I did what I could, but neither of them made it.'

'Who were they?'

'Baxter Elkins and Kid McCoy.'